A
Death
in
Florence

A Novel

Bruce Moss

Cover photograph: courtesy of Edoardo Busti on Unsplash
Designed by Felicia Cedillos
Composed in Sabon 11.25/14.25

A Death in Florence

*To the memory
of my dear son Greg
lost to cancer*

Chapter One

On the morning of the last twenty-four hours of his life, Dr. Anders Jason Croft, respected Professor of Medieval Studies, is asleep. He is not a young man, or even middle-aged. For him those years have fled. Years ago he might have been asleep in one of many hotels, wherever his work or his instinct took him. Now retired, he travels only when necessary.

It is barely dawn when percussive tones of music strike his ears. Barely awake, he wonders if it is Kate at her piano, playing arpeggios. But it is not piano music. Somewhere, bells are ringing. Swimming up through his morning torpor, he tries to identify them. Are they the University chapel bells calling him to class?

But the timbre of these bells is different from those at the University. And there are more of them. He now realizes the bells are repeating a few notes from a Bach Cantata. They are stabbing at his brain like an ice pick. It is so early. Bits and pieces of a dream he's just had are assembling themselves. It was a threatening dream, one that still has his stomach clenched in fear. A rough Tuscan voice had growled in his ear...*ma San Bartolomeo t'accompagnera...*

Anders lurches fully awake. Who is this San Bartolomeo who will accompany him? Accompany him where? The light shining through the white gauze curtains is blinding, even through

Anders' half-closed eyelids. Isn't San Bartolomeo Italian for Saint Bartholomew? Wasn't he one of Jesus's disciples? Or did the voice mean, *Fra* Bartolomeo, who painted the famous frescoes at the turn of the sixteenth century? Perhaps better to have a dead saint by your side than a dead artist. And the dream? His being promised a lady with a golden face, one who lives in a temple on a hilltop? A phrase floats into memory... *if dreams dreamt close to dawn are true...then little time will pass until...*

Anders knows the ancients believed that dreams dreamt close to dawn were prophetic. But right now he needs to know the time, to orient himself in the real world. Why is it so hard to turn his head to check the bedside clock? It isn't just a stiff neck; it's as though his nerves have forgotten how to send their impulses from his brain to his neck muscles. The wires are down. He must get a grip on himself. His left hand makes it to his skull but his right makes it only to his collarbone. God, he thinks, not another stroke. He works the fingers of his left hand against his right temple and pulls his head to the side, far enough to see out of the corner of his left eye. He can see there is no clock. Instead of his familiar cherry wood bed stand there is an unfamiliar white one painted with a blue floral design. He releases his head and lets his arm flop on the bed beside him. Where could he be?

The bells unleash a cascade as if in answer. Something about the clarity of the tones, their pitch, the way the air in the room vibrates. He remembers: Florence. The Hotel Lilia. The bells must be those of Santa Maria Novella, not the primitive ones of the 12th-century Santa Trinita nearby, the latter tolling at seven every morning with its clunky single bell. He is in Florence, the city of Dante, his spiritual home. All will be well. The October light will flash off the River Arno's rippling surface as the water follows its passage though the gauntlet of arched bridges. The light will bless the city's hill-edged sea of red tile roofs and the towering white and green marble of the Duomo's cathedral walls. It will bless the Florentines and even the tourists sitting in the Piazza Signoria sipping their creamy hot chocolate. Will the October light bless him, Anders Croft, as he strolls through the city's old center with Sebastiano, the concierge he has known over the years? If so, all will be well.

But why isn't Kate stirring, surely awakened by the bells? He's caught no murmur, no whisper of her breathing, no movement in the bed. He tries to turn his head to the right to see her, but again his neck muscles simply aren't working this morning. His body feels heavy. And yet his left arm seemed to work. He stretches it across his chest to try to touch her, but he can't reach far enough. It's time to cry out, to wake her. He opens his mouth and speaks, yet out comes a gurgle. He closes his mouth, ashamed. That was not his voice. A man knows his own voice, and that was not it. That was the choking of a dying animal. With luck, Kate didn't hear it.

The bells begin a kind of syncopation as they rock back on themselves with longer and longer pauses. Finally they're mute. He lies there in the new silence and tries to assemble how and why he got to Florence. He remembers uncomfortable hours in a plane, his legs and feet swelling, hurting as if they were locked in a vise. There was a long taxi ride from the airport into Milano through an early morning fog that hugged the ground. He recalls stopping the taxi at the city's gingerbread cathedral where inside, to the right of its altar, stood the statue of San Bartolomeo, his face serene though he has been flayed alive, his skin draped over his shoulder like a serape blanket. That was the name in his dream. San Bartolomeo. And what does this martyred saint mean to him?

At the train station the Roma people had attacked him at the steps, cursing him when he refused them money, pushing their sheets of cardboard up against him to conceal their thieving hands rooting through his pockets. Later, through the window of the train to Florence, he had watched float past him the small stucco houses, the Matchbox cars on the *autostrada*, the golden fields lined with mulberry trees.

Had Kate been with him on the train? Or on the plane? He feels a wave of terror, then guilt. Has he lost her along the way? He gathers his strength, heaves himself up onto his left elbow, twists to his right, and falls back. In that instant he has seen that there is no Kate. How can that be?

Decades ago he had been in Italy with Kate midway through his year's sabbatical to research an obscure figure in Dante's verse. Kate, at thirty-eight, was trying to forge a link to her interrupted career as a concert pianist. A scene unfolds in his brain. He and Kate are in their four-door Alfa Giulia on the *autostrada* approaching a tunnel. She has said something to him, something insistent about the fight they'd had the night before. But she can do nothing to ease his anger at her betrayal. He jerks the wheel and pulls out to pass, blind, a double-trailer truck grinding along excruciatingly slowly. A car comes straight at them, closing too quickly to avoid. There is nowhere to go, he twists the wheel…

All he knows of the head-on collision was in the police report, and in the statement of the truck driver. Anders has no recollection of it. His sense of the words he and Kate exchanged just before the accident is his own construction based on the fight they'd had. He recalls the doctor after the accident, the domed Tuscan forehead creased with worry lines, the brown eyes sorrowful at his hospital bedside as he expressed his condolences: *"Con mio grande dispiacere…"*

He stares at his room's ceiling in horror, as he did in the

hospital all those years ago. He is alone. And gradually he feels a different, perplexing fear, in the face of what? How could he have thought that Kate, thirty years later, was still next to him?

Anders has managed to make it to the bathroom to the toilet, and he now glowers at himself in the mirror. He understands that he must have suffered another stroke—a small one this time. A TIA, as his doctor back in Arizona called it. Transient something or other. Transient ischemic attack—that was it. Nine times as likely to have the Big One after one of these little bastards. The face staring back at him is not chiseled and handsome as it was in years past. Since the big stroke it is off-kilter, right cheek and jaw-line sagging, right eyelid drooping. His skin, once ruddy with health, is ashen. A few strands of silvery hair straggle down his forehead. His ears seem to sprout from the sides of his skull like mushroom caps. His Adam's apple works up and down under the ropes of his throat. Yet the facial asymmetry gives his features an oddly roguish character. His electric-blue eyes and the disdainful lift of his eyebrows still hint at his life's long string of bedroom conquests. Even the full lips that Kate loved still have something of their soft, bruised quality.

He opens those lips to speak but they only quiver. Finally, the words come out: "Anders, you are going to be fine. Absolutely...damned...fine. You hear?" The muddied words sound alien to his ear, as if an alternate voice is speaking. He has to pull himself up by his bootstraps as he has many times during his solitary years. He began doing it after Kate's death, after he got out of the hospital, his fractures slowly healing, when he had to set aside her ghost, settle her affairs, and look after the children. When he found that the lithium didn't help his black-dog depression, he took up cigarettes and a daily half bottle of brown whiskey. Later, after Anna and Thomas were grown, he tapered off to a pipe and only a stiff drink or two in the evening, his routine for decades until his stroke.

He gives his reflection a nod and whispers, "Not bad, after all these years, considering a stroke and a half." He attempts a wink but fails. He tries to stand straight, tall and proud, his shoulders thrown back, as in the past. And just then, tilting his head and raising an eyebrow, an affectation from younger years, yes, he could swear he felt Kate's presence, felt she'd come up behind him. He feels the pressure of her body against his back, the sense of her arms around him, something she did occasionally when he was shaving. "My distinguished, narcissist Professor," she would murmur with affectionate irony.

He shakes off the illusion, a chill flying up his spine. Is Kate his lady of the golden face? Was his dream a mirroring of their time in this city, especially when they visited the Church of San Miniato on the high hill?

"Croft, you're strong," he growls to himself, "*strong!*" He must record the dream in his journal right away before he forgets it. The very act of copying it down will purge it of any disturbing energy.

Back in his bedroom he searches through his suitcase and canvas carry-on bag. After several minutes he realizes he has left his journal in the drawer of his desk in Arizona. He could ask Anna to send it, but they had not parted on the best of terms. No, he can always buy a writing tablet at one of the stalls that line the Piazza della Repubblica.

With infinite effort he dresses, pulling on his gray cavalry-twill trousers, his tan shirt, his gray V-neck sweater, and his socks. He steps into his favorite pair of aging but polished Guccis. Finally he dons the venerable beige Harris tweed jacket he bought on a trip to England so many years ago, fresh out of college, its lining replaced twice.

He will now have to telescope his world down to the taking of one single step at a time to get himself out of his room, down the stairs, along the hallway past the sitting room, and past the breakfast room. There, the other guests, digging into their soft-boiled eggs, sipping their coffee or tea, may glance up at him as he makes his way. Each step will be an adventure, in his present state, until he reaches the front desk. There he will finally lower himself onto the *banco* and wait patiently for Sebastiano to take him out for the promised walk.

With grim focus he unlocks his room door with his good left hand and pulls it open. He pulls out the key, weighted with its heavy rectangular brass plate, and stares at the engraved number: 6. No, it is upside down. It is a 9.

He steps into the hallway, turns, and locks the door behind him. And why *did* they give him room No. 9? Is the hotel staff honoring a Dante scholar—shades of the Ninth Circle? It is a dubious honor for one not so far from death. He reaches into the pocket of his jacket, absent-mindedly testing its capacity to carry the heavy key. He discovers, of all things, a milk bone. Only yesterday—it seems impossible—he was going to give it to Cleo, the German Shepherd belonging to his neighbor back home in Arizona. Sweet Cleopatra, who waits for him at his door each morning for her treat. She did not show up this morning when the airport shuttle came for him. He left too early, he supposes.

As he negotiates the hallway, his mind wanders back over the last month: the arrival of Anna, having just flown in from Ohio. Redheaded, red-eyed and pale, she had announced that she had left her husband and that she and the two children needed to move in with him while she searched for a place to live.

"But my place is too small for all of you, Anna" he'd said, once he overcame the shock of seeing her on his doorstep. "It's only an eleven hundred square foot *casita*. Why didn't you write that you were coming? I could have found you something else."

"So, you're shutting us out?" she replied, fighting back tears. Her hazel eyes—Kate's— blazed at him. The boy and the girl frowned up at him as if he were a cold, unfeeling stranger. "The way you shut out Mother?" Anna said, the tears now rolling down her cheeks.

He had looked at her carefully, this woman with the curly, cinnamon-colored hair, the prominent forehead of her mother, the white cotton turtleneck, the jeans, the worn brown leather jacket; her expression demanding yet supplicating, fierce yet vulnerable, intelligent, pleading. Pleading for what? What did she want from him—what *has* she wanted from him all these years?

"Isn't it time?" she'd said. "All the years you've never shown remorse?"

Yes, in the dark months afterwards he had described the accident on the *autostrada* to Anna and to Thomas as it was reported to him. He had wanted to confess it to ease his own pain—and his conscience. Whatever he'd said hadn't been enough for Anna. She had heard the fight the night before and she had come to her own conclusions. Was she on his Arizona doorstep, her eyes burning, to avenge her mother? No angel, Kate, but he *had* loved her. Had she insisted on her own love just before the crash? Would she have tried to have him admit *his* love in the wake of the previous night's battle? Could he have done that, given her betrayal?

Through his grief and shock in the hospital, Anders had wondered who had picked up Anna and Thomas at school, who had told them what had happened. Would Gabriela, their cook, feed them and take care of them?

Later, there was the tearful packing-up, the abandoning of the house in Greve-in-Chianti, and Kate left behind in the cemetery. She had seemed to smile back at him from her picture on her tombstone—the photo an Italian custom—her dark eyebrows raised in irony, as if asking why she was here in this cemetery, of all places. It was a picture he himself had taken when they were first engaged. Finally, after weeks in the hospital, there had been the trip back to America, trying in his desolation to be a parent, the children distrustful of the new housekeeper. Anna never forgave him, a sentiment he returned, though unfairly and for different reasons.

In the end he accepted Anna and the children into his Arizona *casita*, though he resolved to leave as soon as possible rather than bury himself in a corner and drink himself to death with brown whiskey amid the chaos. Better to flee and leave the residue of his life—the *casita*, the money in the bank, the stocks in the brokerage account—to Anna and her children as final payment of the debt she felt he owed. Better to take some of the money and fly to Florence, perhaps to die an exile like Dante and be buried in the lonely village cemetery that held Kate's grave.

He couldn't admit to Anna he was escaping her and the children. He told her he was finally going to investigate the same scholarly detail in Dante's verse on which he'd hitched his sabbatical to Florence, with her mother, so many years ago. He was going to search out the historical Alessio Interminei, assigned by Dante to the *Inferno's* Eighth Circle, along with the courtesan Thaïs, for the sin of Flattery.

Yes, there is that word, *flattery*. Hadn't honeyed words been an occasional sharp chisel in his own toolbox of persuasion? How otherwise does one ascend the academic ladder, without the occasional use of charm and a kind word to a superior?

Having re-pocketed the milk bone, perhaps a talisman for the future, Anders continues walking. His knees are rubbery and he might as well be descending the Matterhorn in bedroom slippers. Best not to tempt Fate by hurrying under such circumstances. Humility has its necessary place, and not only in Purgatory. A sick old man with a gimpy leg should probably be somewhere safe, but in his condition nowhere is safe. He needed to escape Anna and her children, but again, why did he flee to Florence? Did he not also come here to reacquaint himself with the man who was once Anders Jason Croft? To relive those younger years that sing to him from every crack and crevice of the city? To recover a self that is being lost, synapse-by-synapse, within his own brain?

Step by uncertain step, he makes his way down the hall past the large, empty *salotto* where brilliant tapestries and heavy antique leather couches and chairs invite hotel guests to sit and read. Henry James's *Italian Hours,* Goethe's *Italian Journey,* and E.M Forster's Italian novels sit among others on those shelves. Readers may fantasize that if they listen they might hear the clop of horses' hooves and the grind of carriage wheels on the once-cobbled pavement of the Via Tornabuoni below.

As Anders approaches the entrance to the hotel dining room, he hears the clink of silverware and the murmur of voices. He can smell hints of coffee, of bacon-like *pancetta*, of fresh-baked glazed pastry. Anders draws himself up as best he can. He glances at the diners, at his potential audience. Yes, there they are, men and women betraying that morning bleariness, dressed in today's obligatory jeans and open-collared shirts, perched on chairs before tables set with white linen. He could be there, mouthing learned facts of medieval history in professorial style. If the subject turned contemporary, he could deplore America's international barbarism—the sort of rote recitations that were crucial to wending his way through academia's labyrinth.

He has no stomach for breakfast himself, in fact feels nausea at the idea. As he turns away, his shoe catches the edge of the hall's ancient Karastan rug, and he stumbles. He might have fallen, except for the Renaissance chest his flailing hand—barely missing a crystal vase filled with red and white lilies—grabs at the last moment. With agonizing slowness he pulls himself upright and shoots a humiliated glance toward the dining room. Not one face chattering in the elegant wood-walled refectory has turned his way. He is relieved yet resentful. Nobody has noticed him. Turning his back on the diners, he focuses on an Alinari print portraying in detail the Florence of the year 1500. The print is so familiar. He glances right, then left, almost as if Kate might appear.

In the old days, including the early weeks of his year's sabbatical, he and Kate stayed at the Lilia. It was exactly here one morning, in the year before the Great Flood, that they stood as he pointed out to her the famous buildings in this Fratelli Alinari print.

"If Dante had been able to see this print in 1300," he told her, "the poet would have recognized only two of its buildings. First was the Baptistry, where Dante himself was baptized. The second was the Church of San Miniato al Monte, gazing down on the city from its hill to the southeast. The cathedral and its bell tower—the Duomo and its Campanile—did not yet exist."

"My very own Professor—so erudite!" Kate whispered with a cunning smile. Whenever he produced streams of obscure facts, and she judged him a bit full of himself, she liked to give him a gentle poke in the ribs.

"Actually," he recalls telling her, "Dante composed many of his poetic *sestine* while watching the laying of the Duomo cathedral's foundation as he sat on a nearby piece of ruined stone. That stone, known as Dante's *sasso,* is still there."

She had been in good spirits that day. Upon waking to the Florentine sunshine streaming into their room, they had made long and luxurious love. They had then gone down and gobbled breakfast, flushed and alive, sparring good-naturedly.

He can still see her as she was, after they awakened that May morning, as he paused on his way to the shower. She lay, drowsy, turned on her right side toward the window's sun, her long left leg flexed over her outstretched right, her chestnut hair a dark halo on the sheet, the light playing along the edge of her body, as she gazed—at what? The sun? Thinking what? Was she lost in memories of the days and nights of a languid autumn when they were just out of college, when they first fell in love with this city, prompting their return years later?

He stares at the Alinari print, frustrated that he can picture her so vividly, yet can't clearly recollect *her* after all these years, the Kate who *was.* She has somehow evolved into a person as little known to him as the living Beatrice was little known to Dante—the two Florentines' paths crossing so few times, so few words exchanged.

Anders shakes his head. Will he visit the cemetery? He could rent a car. No, it is enough to know that Kate is close by, within forty minutes' travel. He takes another step down the hallway toward the Lilia's small but elegant lobby, where Sebastiano will be expecting him.

Chapter Two

Having delivered his room key to Sebastiano at the desk, Anders sits on a *banco*, waiting for the concierge to finish his shift. When Anders had phoned from Arizona for his reservation, it had been fifteen years since his last stay. Yet Sebastiano had recognized his voice right away. How wonderful it was for an old man like him to have his heart warmed by such a welcome.

Anders contemplates the spacious lobby, so familiar to him. Its Victorian furnishings have always lent it an atmosphere of bygone Anglo-Saxon gentility. The hotel La Lilia occupies the top three floors of a 13th century palazzo, and has for two hundred years catered mainly to the English. Its historic ambience is one of the reasons Anders returns to it—that, and its central location. He is also drawn by the memories he has accumulated over the years. He thinks of Kate and the children, of course, but also, after the *autostrada* accident, the women he brought to see the sights. They were young ladies whose company and intimacy—their warm bodies stretched out for him on La Lilia's sheets—he recollects now with a mixture of pleasure and bitter nostalgia.

Anders always admired the ingenuity with which the hotel grafted onto its south side a narrow, five-story structure with its two elevators for guests and baggage. For the more athletic guests the original twenty-five foot flight of broad stone steps was retained. The stairway and the elevators converge at the top on wide glass doors that open into the hotel lobby, where Sebastiano or another of the staff sits behind a high mahogany desk, checking guests in and out.

An ancient Shirvan rug, geometrically patterned in faded blues, greens, reds and ivory, the only one Anders has known there, leads guests the length of the lobby past old bookshelves and chests set along the long wall. The scent of old books, antique furniture and aging leather mingles with the fragrance from vases of stargazer lilies, brilliant blue delphiniums, yellow and orange astromeria, and white gladioli.

Anders watches a middle-aged couple check in. The husband, tall and overweight in a brown wool sweater and rumpled beige corduroys, clenches a pipe between his teeth. He is struggling to stuff papers that Sebastiano has just given him into the pocket of a jacket draped over his arm. The wife, elegant with her streaked blonde hair and modest makeup, is wearing a beige pantsuit and a sky-blue blouse, a string of pearls at her throat.

As they approach, probably groggy from lack of sleep and jet lag, the wife gives Anders a glance, the sort of brief assessment she might have given a piece of the hotel's antique furniture. Anders lifts an eyebrow and gives her a mischievous smile. In that brief instant he feels the hint of an electric current pass between them. Her eyes linger for a moment on his. She breaks into the hint of a smile. As she passes he can tell she must feel his eyes on her by the new lilt to her step, the swing of her hips. Anders' imagination spins their marital story—their original lovers' fire turned long ago to banked ashes and the staid comfort of routine. Such a woman, in his experience, is ripe for the kind of fling that awakens her slumbering desire.

Anders shifts his bony rump on the hard *banco*. He glances over at Sebastiano, his vision skewed as his right eye lags in the maneuver. He studies the bald head, the wire-rim reading glasses, the face of a man without expression as he briskly sorts documents on his desktop. It strikes him for the first time that the austere appearance of this man he has known for so long, now past middle age, would easily suit a Cardinal of the Roman Church. All that are missing, Anders thinks, are the flowing crimson robes and skullcap.

In the years that Anders has stayed at the Hotel Lilia, the concierge has been engaging and helpful whenever any need arose. What they have in common are an acquaintance built from Anders' repeated visits, and a shared love of Dante's verse. Sebastiano has made a historical study of the poet's beloved Beatrice Portinari, a project that has become almost an obsession. He has tracked her short life, beginning with her childhood in the Portinari's house on the Via del Corso, where nine-year-old Dante first met her, writing later in moving verse that he had met in her a god stronger than he, one who would come to rule over him. Why does the memory of that meeting, Anders wonders, provoke such a pang in his heart?

As he waits for the concierge to go out for their walk, he is not impatient. For one thing, Anders is still assessing his own physical state. He leans forward and examines his legs. Who knows how they will function down on the streets after his attack? As if to test, he stretches them out in front of him, exerting extra effort with the balky right one.

He sighs and shifts his eyes to two oil paintings on the wall opposite that he has come to know over the years. In the upper one is a nobleman on horseback, splendidly dressed in pearl-white on Easter morning. He is being ambushed as he clatters over the Ponte Vecchio. Anders can almost hear the pounding of the hooves as they thunder over the original wood planks of the bridge. One assassin has leapt and buried his dagger in the nobleman's chest. Blood spurts from the wound. The painting, Anders knows, enacts the vengeance of the Amidei clan in attacking the elegant rider for having jilted an Amidei maiden. Failure in those times to take a slighted family's pride into account could be fatal.

Thinking back, Anders would rather have spent his time researching medieval Florentine culture than teaching students, which was often a chore. And yet there *were* those moments when his heart leapt at the chance to give certain of his female students individual help after class. One ghostly face floats up before him. Flirtatious, blonde and blue-eyed, the daughter of a successful Savannah trial lawyer, the apple of her daddy's eye, Niven Stewart erased for a time all Anders' annoyance with the tedium of teaching. In his late forties at the time, he would have jilted any betrothed and faced any number of Amidei assassins on that ancient bridge if only to possess that young woman.

Anders shifts his attention to the lower painting. Swords flash in the sunlight while warhorses, nostrils flaring, rear and careen against the spring backdrop of a pastoral area east of Florence. It is the Battle of Campaldino in June of 1289, pictured at the moment the Florentines led the cavalry charge that routed the army of the city of Arezzo. Dante the warrior-poet knew well the valley where the battle was fought. What was he thinking as his squadron of cavalry galloped over green fields near his own family's landholdings? Did he wonder if he would ever again see his beloved Beatrice, wonder if his ambition to be the world's greatest poet would drain with his blood into the fresh June fields, soaking the wild asparagus his servants gathered at that time of year?

Anders shakes his head as he recalls Dante's contempt for

those who refuse to choose sides, *"Questi sciaurati...,"* those wretches who, living, never were alive, who chose expedience over belief, convenience over principle. Staring at the Campaldino canvas, Anders asks himself when *he* ever stepped out of the shadows when risk and principle were highest, to forge for *himself* a place among men. He glances around him. Doesn't this lobby, this way station between La Lilia and the world outside, doesn't *it* have the feel of an anteroom to Hell? It was St. John of the Apocalypse who wrote, *"Because thou art lukewarm, neither hot nor cold, I will spue thee from my mouth."*

Anders feels a headache coming on. He leans forward and cradles his face in his hands, hands that now smell of the *banco*'s old leather. He works his feet underneath the low, hard bench and leans back. An absurd rivalry claws at him. What, after all, was so admirable about the character of this Florentine he's spent much of a career studying, this poet who consigned enemies *and* friends to their fates in *La Commedia*? What of the poet's own sin of pride? When Florence tried to decide who should negotiate for the city with Pope Boniface VIII, wasn't it Dante, elected Prior by the Florentines, who announced: "If I go, who stays? If I stay, who goes?" In his own eyes he was indispensable.

Again, was he, Anders, ever a warrior for a cause instead of living only for himself? The notion offends his conscience, the way coarse wool irritates the tender skin of his torso. Yet had he not been at the center of Vietnam-era peace marches that tore into the administrations that sent young men to their deaths?

Inculcating his students with moral fervor: surely that counted. Niven, for instance, her blonde hair shimmering, was one of his initiates. Such passion he ignited in that warm young body, such righteous indignation after Watergate and the Nixon-Ford criminal deal. Even after Vietnam, The Cause presented such a welcome conduit for seduction. How many times in road-trip motels did he, his heart pounding amid clouds of incinerated marijuana, remove those tie-dyed jeans of hers? Who denies that principle and pleasure can co-exist?

Anders stretches out his once elegant shoes before him and inspects them. He notices a spot on the right heel that he missed when he so doggedly polished them yesterday in Arizona. He laughs sourly. Where was Dante's virtue, leading his shock troops at Campaldino to join in killing seventeen hundred citizens of Arezzo in a single battle? Did *he* rouse the Florentines to march for peace? As City Prior, did *he* ever rage against war?

Anders grips the *banco* and clenches his teeth. Why shouldn't a professor fighting to retain tenure defend himself? What files shouldn't he ransack to discover the identity of his enemies? Given the chance, wouldn't Dante have slit the throats of those who exiled him? Wouldn't he have strangled those who self-righteously opposed his recall from exile—the same ones who confiscated his property?

Anders slumps. It is no use. Dante is for the ages. He, Anders, will disappear like a pebble tossed in a pond. This lobby, this anteroom, is just the place for him, waiting in the shadows for death.

He turns and glares at Sebastiano, as if he is to blame. Oddly, the concierge has also been staring at *him*, apparently lost in thought. Sebastiano glances at the clock on the wall. It is ten o'clock. He returns to writing in his reservations book. Footsteps approach from the outer hallway and a young man in a black hotel uniform enters. Sebastiano rises and exchanges words with him before walking over to Anders.

"*Vuol fare*…shall we go for our stroll, *Professore?*" Sebastiano begins. "But you don't look well."

"*Mi sento abbastanza bene,*" Anders says, rising unsteadily. "I feel pretty well, but I slept poorly last night," he continues in Italian. "Just the same, it is a pleasure to speak Italian with you this morning."

"I hope you weren't kept awake. We had guests after midnight." The concierge delivers the word for midnight, *mezzanotte,* with a slight hunch of the shoulders. His face expresses apology but his delivery is neutral and velvet-smooth.

"No, no. I would have slept well, but I had a bad dream."

"Too bad, on your first night. Let me change into clothes fit for strolling," the concierge says with a smile, "and then we will walk, and you tell me about this dream of yours."

As Anders reseats himself his eyes follow Sebastiano's back as he walks rapidly down the hall to a doorway marked *"PRIVATO,"* the entrance to a room that admits staff only. It is a room that even now, all these years later, pulls at Anders' memory, drawing him back in time—*eyes of liquid silver, her laugh startled and innocent, yet questioning.* She was the younger cousin of Sebastiano, so long ago. That sliver of door he glimpses at this angle from his *banco*—it brings on such a sudden sensation of joy. But the image of a blushing young face glancing up from her studies brings also a slight prick of shame.

Disconcerted, he shifts position on the hard leather of the bench. Why does memory, he wonders fiercely, torment the old, calling up one's youth in such high gloss, sadistically honoring that early stage of life that glowed before experience and time worked their corruption? What would Kate think if she could see him now, all these years later, doddering in the lobby of the hotel she knew so well? Would she recognize him? He shudders. How that simple door painted *"PRIVATO"* mocks his years.

Sebastiano reappears in minutes wearing a leather-buttoned beige cardigan, freshly pressed gray wool trousers, and a pair of polished brown shoes. Italians, Anders muses, are rarely to be seen in public appearing inelegant. He rises, Sebastiano takes his elbow, and together they walk toward the large glass double doors of the outer hallway. Things are better now, with someone to steady him.

In moments they are in the hallway, waiting for an elevator. It is quiet. Both elevators are apparently being held below by newly arriving guests. Anders recalls when he chose this hotel himself so many years ago. It had certainly seemed appropriate for a Dante scholar, set as it is at the unlikely intersection of the Via dell'Inferno and the Via del Purgatorio.

Even in his uncertain state his spirits are improved by the prospect of a walk with Sebastiano, who has become almost a friend over the years. One can confide things to a hotel concierge in a foreign land that one might not confide to others. Of course there will always be a distance between them that is appropriate between a hotel's guest and its staff. It would be naive to think that Sebastiano has no regard for the generous tip Anders will give him at the end of his stay.

"It will be pleasant outside," Sebastiano says. "Mild for October."

"Mild is always appreciated." Anders, leaning on Sebastiano's arm, has most of his weight on his left foot. "Age prefers the temperate to the cold." He smiles at such an obvious aphorism. "But let me tell you about this dream of mine," he murmurs. "First, there was an inn..."

"The Hotel Lilia?"

Anders shakes his head. "No, it was a resort at the foot of a mountain. I was paying the bill, ready to leave, when the innkeeper told me about a beautiful lady with a golden face who lived in a temple at the top of the mountain." His eyes are on the flickering red numbers that track the elevator. "Instead of a temple I found up there only a forest of dead, twisted trees, with a storm threatening. And instead of a woman with a face of gold I found an ancient woman waiting for me. She seemed to be a witch—*una strega*."

"That innkeeper was playing with you, *Professore*." Light dances in the concierge's eyes. "Are you sure he wasn't me?"

Anders glances at him. "Not you, Sebastiano. You never mislead me. You are not malevolent. It seemed clear that this innkeeper was sending me to my death."

"Ah, there's the difference. I would not send you to your death. Nor mislead you. But I am clairvoyant. Therefore," he says, lifting his eyes upward, "I predict that this afternoon you will meet a remarkable woman. She has no face of gold, but she is beautiful and she is real."

Anders grins. "I certainly prefer that kind of prediction."

"But you don't know what woman I am thinking of," Sebastiano says, looking at him out of the corner of his eye.

"Nevertheless."

An elevator opens in front of them. An American couple with their three young children explode out. The children are teasing one another, pinching and pushing, and the stylishly dressed, dark-haired mother hisses at them as they jostle past. The short, plump father smiles wearily and shakes his head apologetically. The other elevator opens, and a porter struggles out with the family's luggage.

Sebastiano holds the door open for Anders, they enter the elevator, and the concierge pushes a button. The door slides closed, and the elevator begins its descent. Anders is disturbed by the slightly rank, moist odor left by young active bodies, as if such animal spirits are an affront to his own ebbing vitality. Did his Anna and Thomas smell like that when they were little? Not that he can remember.

"How could you tell that your innkeeper was malevolent, *Professore,* and intent on murdering you, rather than merely misleading you?"

"Yes, the dream. The innkeeper reminded me of an ex-Nazi in an American movie some years ago. He seemed to be promising me a reward of a lady with a golden face, but he was actually damning me." He glances at Sebastiano. "Like an angry, Old Testament God."

"*Un Dio arrabbiato?* And so what happened?"

"When I got to the top I just stared at the blasted woods and the storm, feeling tricked and frightened."

"Were they like the woods in which Dante lost himself at the beginning of *La Commedia?*" the concierge asks matter-of-factly.

"If anything they were more like the thorn trees in the Inferno's Seventh Circle, the ones bearing the souls of the suicides."

The concierge shakes his head. "If you want my opinion, *Professore*, the spirit of Dante entered your sleeping body and whispered of Florence. The city of his birth is the lady of the golden face. The poet envies you. In your great good fortune you have returned to the city that was out of his reach in all his years of exile."

Anders smiles. "*Bravo*, Sebastiano—an excellent interpretation. But what of the old lady? The *strega?*"

The concierge rubs his chin. "She must be your soul," he says thoughtfully, "that has accompanied you every step of your life's journey."

"Not bad, Sebastiano. Still, I would have preferred a young, beautiful soul."

The concierge shrugs. "What's to be done? She could only be young and beautiful if you were young and handsome."

Anders laughs. "Unfair."

The elevator comes to rest and Sebastiano holds the door open. "And that was the end of your dream?"

Anders limps out into the broad corridor. "Now I remember—when I woke up to the bells of Santa Maria Novella, there was a voice speaking in Tuscan dialect. '*Non hai paura*—fear not, San Bartolomeo will be with you."

"That is all?"

Anders slowly nods. "The only San Bartolomeo I know is the statue in the Milano Cathedral. He stands there, having been flayed, his skin draped over his shoulder. You can see his veins and fascia."

Sebastiano sighs. "He was, of course, one of the twelve apostles, *Professore*. He was flayed and crucified in Greater Armenia by King Astyages. It is said that they lowered his cross and, when he was *in extremis*, they beheaded him."

"Grim stuff. How do you know this?"

The concierge seems to contemplate the corridor's marble floor. "My parents told me. You see, my full name is Sebastiano Bartolomeo Donati. I wanted to know after whom I and my great uncle were named. I looked into it further and found that San Bartolomeo preached not only in Armenia, but in India, Mesopotamia, Persia, and Egypt. A town here in the Chianti, San Barberino d'Elsa, celebrates his feast day every five years."

Anders feels dizzy, as though a character of his own making has come alive before his eyes. "What motivated you to dig all that up?"

"Simply curiosity. I found that San Bartolomeo is the patron saint of children. It is why my parents included his name in mine, no doubt to protect me. Of the rest they knew nothing."

"Just as I knew nothing of him," Anders murmurs. "Yet I dreamed this martyr placed me under his protection."

"You remembered the statue in Milano. Perhaps that was enough."

"A gruesome death."

Sebastiano shrugs. "A Christian martyr allows his skin to be torn away, baring his soul to the world. Nothing hidden. What is gruesome to us is glorious for a martyr."

The concierge takes Anders by the elbow and guides him the length of the corridor, through the great open doors and out onto the crowded sidewalk of the Via Tornabuoni. "Think, *Professore*. It is Saturday, October 29th, the Day of Joyful Mysteries on the Holy Catholic Calendar."

Chapter Three

As they step out of the doorway onto Via Tornabuoni, Anders already feels drained. His right leg isn't cooperating, as if the cords that connect his hip, knee and ankle have jumped their pulleys. But sunlight floods his eyes. He hears stray chatter in Tuscan dialect. His soul seems to awaken. Once again he feels the joy of being in this city. In moments they are at the tiny Piazza Santa Trinita, where three roads dating from ancient times intersect. One, the Via delle Terme, led the dusty and weary to the nearby baths two thousand years ago.

Baths. Anders recalls that Kate was fond of long hot ones, reclining nobly and luxuriously, the scent of bath-oil rising from the foam around her. She used to wonder if the Roman baths were still below here—covered over by the layers of time, ready for the steaming water. Did Niven love baths too? He can't remember. Oh yes, he can still hear her giggling in the bath at La Lilia while amid the slipping and splashing he tried to fit his body to hers.

He stares at the tall Column of Justice rising from the Piazza's center a few meters from the Palazzo Spini-Ferroni—the Palazzo Ferragamo to tourists. "Wasn't it Pope Pius IV," he asks, turning to Sebastiano, "who removed that column from the Baths of Caracalla and sent it as a gift to the Medici?"

"Yes, *Professore.*"

"Of course ancient Rome's Caracalla dwarfed anything here."

"Including the number of assignations taking place in its inner chambers, wouldn't you imagine?" the concierge says softly. "Older men's pleasures with *le giovinette*, the young girls?"

Anders gives Sebastiano a quick look. "I thought the sexes were separated."

"Anything was possible in Imperial Rome, *Professore*. For the lustful, one young, well-oiled body, girl or boy, served as well as another. When the statue of Justice was placed atop the column in 1581 it completed the irony, no?"

Anders searches Sebastiano for a sign—of what? The concierge has always kept his comments proper to a long-time client. Not that Anders is a prude—far from it. But Sebastiano is well aware that several of the women he has brought with him to La Lilia over the years were less than half his age. Only his affair with the darling Diana, the concierge's young cousin, was carefully concealed. Diana would never have breathed a word, terrified her cousin might find out. So what is Sebastiano up to? Is he poking fun at an old man on the wane? Does he suspect something after all these years?

They turn left and make their way up the Via Tornabuoni toward the elegant Giacosa, Kate's favorite pastry shop in the old days. Anders still remembers the delicious *torte*, the delicate cakes filled with whipped cream, topped with *fragole di bosco*—tiny wild strawberries.

Anders stops and looks around. "Where is Giacosa, Sebastiano?"

"Gone, *Professore*. Like so many things."

"What a shame. Kate would have been so disappointed."

"No doubt she would have."

They turn ninety degrees and walk east along the wide Via degli Strozzi. Cars and motorbikes hurtle past, forcing Anders to flinch again and again. He is disturbed by the flashy new designer stores along the Strozzi. They were not here the last time. This is not the Florence he knew.

After ten minutes of unsteady progress he and the concierge find themselves in the arcade of the Piazza della Repubblica. Tourists and Florentines hurry past them to its banks, post office, bookstore, newsstands and flower kiosk. Anders notices a young couple standing near the flower kiosk with their two small children. The mother bends over the little girl, warning her in English to stop chasing her little brother around the postcard stand. Anders' head swims and he stumbles; the concierge steadies him.

"Are you all right, *Professore?*"

"Memories, memories," Anders mutters. "They make me dizzy. The year Kate and I and Anna and Thomas lived in Greve, we drove into Florence once a week to shop. After buying groceries on the outskirts we would park here in the piazza. It was allowed in those days." He stops. "Why is my memory of things from three decades ago so incredibly clear, as if they happened only yesterday?"

Sebastiano smiles but says nothing.

"Kate and I used to take the children shopping at UPIM, the department store that used to be over there on the Calimala," Anders says, pointing across the piazza. "Before leaving we would stroll in this arcade. Thomas would beg for a toy car or truck at one of the stands, and Anna would say no, making him cry. Kate would tell Anna to stop being bossy. Before leaving we would buy cut flowers for the house at this same kiosk. Women love flowers, and Kate was no exception." He stops, his palm on his forehead at the force of the memory. "In those days such details seemed so mundane, nothing to pay attention to. But it was life, wasn't it, drifting by unnoticed? Like a breeze down the Arno?"

Sebastiano shakes his head. "*La famiglia*. It must have been sweet to have a son and a daughter," he says. "Especially a daughter. Yours might have reminded you of Beatrice herself. I'll never forget Dante's describing the trembling of his heart when they met as children."

"That was in 1273," Anders says, turning away. "I remember his words."

"No, *Professore*, one would never forget."

"Anyway," Anders continues, "we would include a visit to the Uffizi Gallery to show Anna and Thomas great art. At the time, the courtyard outside the museum was more or less a drug dealer habitat. Once..." He stops and shakes his head. "Once, Thomas asked me why a disheveled young man was lying on the paving stones out there with his eyes closed. You couldn't even tell if he was alive. Thomas seemed so worried, staring, almost as if he could see the future. I told him the young man was sleeping." Anders takes a deep breath. "Little Thomas pulled on my thumb and whispered, 'but Daddy—he's not breathing.'"

Anders stops. Fixed in his mind is a stone tablet, a lonely grave lost somewhere in Seattle, where Thomas lived and died. "Why these hauntings?" Anders mutters.

The concierge takes his elbow. "*Professore*, are you sure you are all right? I know of a doctor not far from here."

Anders glances around him, disoriented and embarrassed. A doctor? Who might put him in a hospital? The only hospital he knows in Florence is Santa Maria Nuova, founded by Beatrice's father, Folco Portinari. There, after the accident on the *autostrada* over thirty years ago, he spent so many weeks recovering. He is not ready for that. A man his age rarely survives hospitals, with their poisonous urine and antiseptics.

"They never got my son Thomas to a hospital," Anders says, beginning to walk, as two loose-limbed youths jostle by, arm in arm. "It was a drug overdose. We hadn't spoken for years." He feels again the sensation, that January day, of his insides collapsing. The voice on the phone from the Seattle Police Department said that Thomas had been dead at least twenty-four hours. The syringe was still hanging from his arm, someone said later—that same little arm he had washed in the tub each evening after Kate's death, after the housekeeper had gone home. Impossible, he had thought. Thomas had just finished a drug rehab program. He had learned that from Anna, since he and his son had not spoken for years.

"Two days after that, I had my first stroke," Anders says.

"*Mi dispiace, Professore*. I am sorry."

The concierge sounds sincere, and Anders stops. "Thomas had injected five times a lethal dose of heroin. It was no accident." A son's revenge? For what? Lack of a father?

They have passed out of the covered arcade into the great open space of the Piazza della Repubblica. The concierge points vaguely at an elegant *gelateria*. "Maybe a cappuccino at Gilli's? It might improve your spirits."

Inside Gilli's it is warm. They are shown to a table in the large inner room, with its wood-paneled wainscoting and creamy figured-plaster ceiling. The smell of espresso and freshly baked pastry, the chatter of the waiters, and the clinking of cups and saucers begin to revive Anders. Tables filled with couples, or men talking business, are ranged along the sides of the room. Only one person sits alone: a woman Anders guesses is in her sixties. Her long gray hair is pinned up in the old fashion, and her pendulous turquoise earrings lend her square, finely boned face a distinct elegance. Her eyes flicker at Anders and Sebastiano, and it flashes through Anders' mind that Kate would not be much older than this woman if she were alive. He smiles at her, and the corners of her mouth turn up faintly before she returns to her book.

Anders glances around the room. On the wall behind their table is a sign advertising the restaurant's availability for weddings. Anders can almost hear Kate's laughter. Visiting Florence before they were married, Kate noticed this same sign. "*Matrimoni!*" she exclaimed. "What a good idea!" She joked that after their wedding ceremony in the old Santa Trinita church they should have a reception here at Gilli's, and invite all the espresso-imbibing Florentine patrons to join them as guests. In the end, they decided on a dawn wedding in San Salvatore al Monte, the church next to San Miniato that overlooks the city. The reception was held a week later at Kate's parents' home in Atlanta.

As he and Sebastiano order cappuccino and breakfast pastry, Anders' mind lingers on the Atlanta reception—the men's morning coats, the women's gowns, the laughter. But he catches the concierge staring at him.

"What's on your mind, Sebastiano?"

The concierge adjusts his silverware and napkin. "Naturally, *Professore*, at your age it is not easy to travel, with the airport security, the long lines, the crowded planes. If I may, what prompted you to visit Florence again at this vulnerable time of your life?"

Anders notes Sebastiano's honest curiosity. "True, I am not in the best of health." He straightens his posture and puffs out his chest, as if to challenge the admission he has just made. He glances at the lady with the pinned-up hair and the turquoise earrings, but she looks away. "Two weeks ago my Arizona *casita's* doorbell rang and there was my daughter, the one you called a Beatrice. She arrived on my doorstep with her children and luggage as if they had dropped out of the sky. There has been a distance between Anna and me ever since her mother died. She has never forgiven me," he mutters, "for the accident. Anyway, she explained that she had left her husband."

"How terrible."

"My daughter is a very unhappy person. She blames every misfortune on the accident that killed her mother. I don't mind saying that I left my *casita* to get away from her, considering the sense of guilt her presence aroused in me. I'd had in mind a slow death by whiskey." He smiles crookedly, unable to use the word "suicide" since losing Thomas. "After I thought about it, I decided why not let her have the *casita*. If I'm to die I'd rather die in a city filled with good memories, not waiting in Arizona for my offspring to shovel me into the ground."

"But surely that is not the case, *Professore*."

"I'm afraid it is." Indeed, six-year-old Anna had understood and remembered much of what Kate shrieked at him that night before her death on the *autostrada*.

Mischief glints in the concierge's eye. "What a shame. I would have thought that you, of all people, would feel blessed with a daughter." His voice trails off. "So you prefer burial here, among us Florentines, such good people? Ah, *Professore*, you know our history. We have our *vendette*, which perhaps we take more seriously than others," he says, his eyes suddenly hard.

"*Vendette?* For what? Who would want to take revenge on me here?"

"*Naturalmente*." The concierge's voice has gone flat. "I mean that anyone, even a good *Professore* of medieval studies, or a harmless concierge, could be hurt by someone seized by a strange impulse."

They are silent as the waiter arrives and sets on their table steaming cups of cappuccino and a plate of four butter-fly-shaped *farfalle* pastry. He slips their check under the ash-tray.

Anders is distracted by the sharply raised voices of an elderly American couple nearby. They seem to be arguing about whether the *porcini* mushrooms appear in the mountains in spring or fall. He supposes he could lean toward the couple and whisper that fresh *porcini* are a late summer delight. But gauging their bitter smiles, he understands that mushrooms probably aren't the point. Arguing is their sport, begun in their twenties as a form of erotic arousal, now continued out of habit, its origin forgotten.

Anders glances at the lady with the turquoise earrings. She, too, has been listening to the couple, her fleeting smile giving her away. Do she and he share a private joke? Her eyes linger on him for a moment before she returns to her book.

"I have no enemies here," Anders says. "Any enemies I had are in America—University enemies." He shakes his head. "But that was long ago."

Again the concierge's eyes light up. "Forgive me, but I find it strange that you did not stay home and make peace with your family—and your enemies."

Anders lifts his cup to his lips with a wobbly left hand, sips, and replaces it on the saucer. "Listen, after escaping the University I thought I had found shelter from the world in my Arizona *casita*: surrounded by the calming desert, losing myself at night in the sound of the wind." He spoons sugar into his cappuccino and stirs it past the foamed milk. "The young can haunt you when they speak for ghosts."

"Haunt you? I never had children, *Professore*, so I don't know. But I would love to have had a daughter. What I have," Sebastiano says, his voice faint, "is a cousin, a dozen years younger than I, whom I have adored since she was a child. I'm sure you remember her."

Anders gives him a quick glance. He couldn't know, could he? *Her eyes bewitching him, like liquid silver, in one so young, behind the staff door with its "PRIVATO."* No, he will not travel down that road that intersects the tragic road, the *autostrada.* "Cousins are perhaps preferable to daughters," he mutters to the concierge.

The concierge examines his *farfalla.* "Is that a question, *Professore*, of experience or taste?"

Again Anders gives him a sharp glance. He decides to let the comment go. *He couldn't know.* He peers around the room, past the square-faced woman with the turquoise earrings, deep in her book. He is searching for glass shelves, common to Italian bars, filled with bottles of cognac, wine, and best of all, grappa. There are none. Two ounces of brandy in his cappuccino would be welcome just now, a late morning medicinal.

Instead, he reaches for more pastry. "As you know," he says abruptly, "at the end, when he was dying, Dante's daughter came to him in Ravenna. It is supposed she was a comfort, but maybe not. Maybe she was an irritant. Maybe she pestered him to swallow his pride, show penance to the Florentine authorities who had exiled him, and come home to his family."

The concierge stares into his cup. "*Professore*, all Italians read Dante in school and know *La Commedia* by heart. But few Americans study him. What led you to do so?"

Anders shrugs. "Without Dante there might have been no Pound, no Eliot. Have you ever read 'The Wasteland?' Who can forget Eliot's using Dante's lines to contrast the fate of active, fraudulent sinners in the Eighth Circle with Prufrock's sin of inaction?"

"Active and inactive sinning?" Sebastiano says with a wry smile. "*There* is a subject for discussion."

Anders gazes up at the immense fan of elongated glass panes forming the top third of the Roman arch over the door that leads to the espresso bar. "To answer your question, my fascination with Alighieri began with my maternal grandmother."

"Your *nonna*?"

"She was born in a small village in the Abruzzi Mountains. She and my grandfather met while he was studying art in Rome after winning the American Academy's Prix de Rome. It was 1911. She was modeling to pay for voice lessons. She always insisted that she modeled only her hands, not her figure. She was very proud," he says.

"Ah, yes, grandmothers tend to be proud," Sebastiano says with a smile. "So your grandfather was American?"

"As a boy in Michigan he was found to have a fine talent for drawing and painting. He grew up to become famous as a muralist in the nineteen twenties and thirties. My *nonna* had a fine singing voice, and it was her ambition that took her from the mountains to Rome to find her fortune as a *coloratura* singer. Years later, when my parents' marriage began to crumble, my *nonna* would visit us. She spoke of Dante's *Commedia*, and the poet's love for Beatrice."

"She must have been a romantic, your *nonna*."

"A disappointed romantic after she and my grandfather eventually divorced. When my grandfather became famous, the ladies chased him, and he did not resist."

Sebastiano shakes his head. "It all makes sense."

"My love of women?" Anders half-smiles. "I eventually discovered my own Beatrice. I was thirteen and her name was

Eleanor. It was at a birthday party. I couldn't take my eyes off her as she demonstrated a sort of trick in a hallway. Perhaps you know it. You stand inside a doorway and press the backs of your hands against the inside of the doorframe for half a minute, then step away. Your arms lift effortlessly from your sides and rise as if by magic. My Eleanor repeated it, as if to convince herself of the sensation. For me she was a blonde angel in a white dress, and her arms were wings. I was stricken. I couldn't get her out of my head. For many months I couldn't sleep, unable to imagine how to approach her."

"And so that is how it all began for you," the concierge muses. "Yet if you had been forty when you met her, the story would have been different, no?"

Anders checks the concierge's face, but it is expressionless. "I would have been older, and less innocent. But my shock of the sight of her beauty would have been the same."

"Indeed? Like Dante when he first saw eight-year-old Beatrice, your heart at the age of forty would have trembled like a flame in the wind—*come una fiamma al vento*?"

What is the concierge driving at? Could he possibly *know* what he did with Diana? Anders' eyes flick over to the lady with the turquoise earrings, who still seems deep in her book. "At any age," he murmurs.

Sebastiano's eyes gleam at Anders from behind his wire-rim glasses. "I adored my young cousin," he says. "I feel the same adoring love when I watch Puccini's *La Boheme*, when Mimi and Rodolfo kiss, when they sing of their joy, and their pain. In those years it was more madness and sweetness than I could take." He gives Anders a level glance. "But my love was pure, *Professore*, chaste and impossible. Like Dante, I adored her from afar. *I still do.*"

Anders is surprised by the concierge's vehemence. "Still?"

"Still."

"Dante was unusual not to lose his passion for Beatrice. You must be an exception, too, Sebastiano. Otherwise when you grew older you might have found someone else with whom to consummate your love."

Something like anger flares across the concierge's features. "I would not betray her so easily. The sacred candle I lit in my heart will burn always."

"Yes, yes," Anders sighs, "but we're not speaking of the Virgin Mary."

"No? Then no matter what you say, you never did experience the love the poet spoke of. Have you forgotten the years he spent hopelessly watching her, several pews behind her during Sunday Mass at the parish church, Santa Margherita de' Cerchi? Was she not his own Virgin Mary?" he asks, his brown eyes moistening behind his lenses.

Anders is taken aback at the concierge's passion. "My friend, you don't think I understand, but I do. Watching Eleanor at our little country church, growing up, it was an epiphany when I discovered her very *birthday*. Even now, no matter what strange or stressful things are going on in my life, it is a sacred day. I imagine her face, and my heart beats fast. I wonder what she is doing, where she lives, tremble to wonder if she is still alive." He stares at the table. "I last saw her when she and I were twenty-one, more than fifty years ago."

The concierge drains his cup and sets it down. "Unfortunately a woman who is a goddess for one man can be treated as a *puttana* by another."

Anders, shocked, narrows his eyes. But the concierge's face is expressionless. He has used the word for whore mildly, with little energy, as if speaking hypothetically. Anders clears his throat. "Of course now, old as I am, when I think of a goddess,

I think of Kate. Surely you remember my wife from our visits over the years, especially when we would stay at La Lilia, before we found the house in Greve?"

Sebastiano toys with his cup. "I remember her well, *Professore.*"

"When she died," Anders murmurs, "she was only thirty-eight, only a little older than Anna is now. It is hard to believe, when I look at the pictures." He sighs and shakes his head. "Our American colleges were near each other, we were lovers, and after my graduation we came here for a few months. I didn't have much money, and I suppose I thought I would stay with her. But her parents arranged for her to stay in the home of a respectable *signora per bene* who lodged only proper young ladies under respectable circumstances, which did not include co-habitation with a lover."

"Appearances and, occasionally, respect." The concierge folds his arms over his chest. "*Professore*, there is something I would like to ask. You have had many conquests of women over the years, some you have only told me about, but others I have seen with my own eyes." He shifts in his chair but keeps his eyes on Anders. "I know how Italians seduce, but you are American, and American men are not known for their ways with women. Business, yes; women, no." His cocks his head. "How would you describe your *tecnica*?"

"My technique?" Anders frowns. Is the concierge mocking him? An Italian asking an American how he seduces? But of course this is Sebastiano, not some Casanova. "I am an old man and my technique is long gone." He glances at the lady with the earrings. She is staring at him intently. It's a bit too far to tell but he imagines the color of her eyes as hazel, like Kate's. He smiles at her. But she does not return his smile, instead she looks away. His face suddenly feels prickly. Is she listening to them?

"But that is not true," Sebastiano says. "I saw the way you smiled at that guest's wife as she walked through the hotel lobby earlier this morning, how it pleased her, and how she returned your smile."

Anders lowers his voice. "It embarrasses me that you say such things. But listen, you are an Italian. Don't pretend Italians aren't professors to the world in these matters."

The concierge's eyes take on a fierce glint behind his wire-rimmed lenses. "Yes, but I want to know how *you* do it."

Sebastiano may be trying to needle him, but that's all right. He will humor him. Anders finishes his cappuccino, sets the cup down and sighs. It will not be the first time he has bragged of his conquests. He rubs his chin thoughtfully. "First of all, I must fall in love with a woman, in love with her own special mystery. At the same time I must feel a spark of my first love for my Eleanor. The woman will have special qualities of her own, but I must feel that original sensation. If I do, then all things are possible, since I will be utterly fascinated, completely absorbed in her." Already he feels his blood rising, whatever Sebastiano's motive in asking him. He glances at the lady with the earrings. She has stopped reading, her gaze fixed in a kind of reverie on a point several feet above Anders' head.

Sebastiano leans back in his chair, arms folded. "You see, you don't sound like an American now. You sound like an Italian."

"I'll assume that to be a compliment. I understand," Anders says. "So, most American men ask a woman out to dinner, and what do they do? They talk about themselves the whole time, their interests, their likes and dislikes, their career successes, true or made up. After an hour the poor woman, unless she's sizing up his earning potential, is bored out of her mind. No, she feels invisible. Or like a prop. She imagines that he would be just that way in bed—vacant, clumsy, self-involved, sensitive as a robot."

The concierge shakes his head. "I'll have to take your word for it."

"Anyway, American women have to be given the right attention to get the best out of them. If I show fascination with her, which is easy if I have fallen for her, then I'm a hero after all those boring, puffed-up egotists. She feels special. Faculty wives in American universities are famously neglected. A little attention, perhaps a few words whispered in her ear followed by a quiet, off-color joke, these work wonders. She can laugh and forget about her fusty professor husband who is too oblivious, too covered with chalk dust to recall that he has a wife."

"And your students?" Sebastiano's smile is almost glassy. He drops his gaze and plays with his spoon. "The young girls?"

Anders sighs. "That is different, Sebastiano. I would never set out to seduce a young girl. That does not mean that I didn't occasionally fall in love with a student. Particularly if she reminded me of Eleanor, or put me into that state that overcame me when I was first in her presence. If I felt I was once again that thirteen-year-old boy, dumbstruck and tongue-tied, I would forget my past ease with women, forget I was ever even married. It is very strange," he says, shaking his head. "With such a student, when I caught sight of her during my lecture, bent over her writing pad, her hair perhaps fallen to one side, writing down the very words I was speaking, I would lose all focus." Anders sighs. "I felt a thrill, a kind of secret connection she was unaware of. She was my angel, with wings," he says. "I experienced a strange mixture of passion and fear," he says, closing his eyes. "It's embarrassing for me to tell you these things, Sebastiano."

The concierge is shifting in his chair, his face flushed. "So you can say in all honesty that you never had sex with a young girl?"

Anders slowly shakes his head. "Sex, you ask? Romance? Love? I can only tell you that I never took advantage of a young woman unless she was a willing partner who loved me as much as I loved her. Women and young girls are not made of stone. Why do you think they read these romance novels, watch movies of love stories, have fantasies of all kinds? I can only say that I never set out to despoil young virgins. My love for them would have precluded such plotting."

"And afterwards? After you have *had* them?"

Anders notices the bite in the concierge's tone. "I refuse to say I *had* these young ladies." He glances away disdainfully. "Afterwards, yes, they will admit, if only to themselves, that they were glad they did not miss out on having their lives heightened by a few moments of passion."

The concierge's expression has gone glum. "While you talked I have been studying that painting on the wall to your right."

Anders turns to look. They are mostly pictures of military parades on the nineteenth century Piazza della Repubblica. But among them is a somber-hued watercolor landscape of an old man sitting on a knoll. He is slumped against a gnarled olive tree, staring into the painted distance at a horse-drawn carriage. The carriage is clearly traveling from a castle that is perched on a far-off hill.

"What does that old man feel?" the concierge asks quietly. "Does he perhaps remember walking along that road in his youth? Might he remember such a carriage riding out of the castle's great gate, and passing him as he walks? Might he have seen in that carriage a lovely young girl, perhaps accompanied by her mother? And if his and the girl's eyes met for the briefest of moments, how would he be able to forget that?"

Anders leans back. "You're a sentimentalist, Sebastiano."

"Perhaps. But if you are a portrait of a realist, I think I prefer my sentimentality."

"Come, Sebastiano. Sentimentality reminds me of Bavarians

singing in beer halls." Anders eyes his companion. "So, how *are* things with you, my old friend?" he asks on impulse. "You seem somehow upset."

Sebastiano eyes Anders askance, as if doubting that his companion does not know. He begins fussing with his paper napkin. "Life has its disappointments, *Professore*. My parents, for instance. As you know, here in Italy we are obliged to care for our parents as long as they live, though with the younger generations everything is changing. *Mia mamma e mio babbo* are in their nineties. As their only child, I live with them and take care of them. They depend on me."

"In America the young kick their old parents into institutions and grab their homes."

"I'm sure you exaggerate. But it may be that way here soon. Of course when *my* parents are gone, I will be the one in an institution—with my *malattia nervosa*." He stares at Anders. "I often wonder what life might have been for me. In the end I am like that old man staring at the castle, dreaming of the girl he glimpsed in his youth. Still, that has been enough."

Anders catches movement out of the corner of his eye. His lady of the earrings has risen, picked up her book, and is about to leave. Her face is coloring—from words she has overheard? From the attention of his repeated glances? She raises her hand to her face, as if to shade it from the light, hiding her eyes from his. Is this the effect he has had on her? She does not look at him as she makes her way across the room, without a glance in his direction, toward the door. *He has lost her.* It is an old sadness she has set off.

Anders sighs. "Sebastiano, do you remember when Dante was weeping over the death of Beatrice, and through his tears he caught sight of the Window Lady pitying him from her high window? He riveted her with his eyes, refusing to let her escape as he rose from where he sat, entered her building, found her bedroom, and..."

"You were not there, *Professore*. Perhaps it was not a cynical seduction. Perhaps they were drawn together honestly, by a common grief."

"That is possible," Anders says, reluctantly surrendering his vision. "You have a good heart, Sebastiano." But he sees that the concierge is pale. "Excuse me. A moment ago you mentioned a *malattia nervosa*."

The concierge leans back in his chair and tips his head to the side. "How shall I say this?" He is silent for a full minute as he studies Anders. "Did you ever read a novel by the Russian, Dostoyevsky, called *The Idiot*? There was a main character, a Prince Myshkin."

Anders understands. Epilepsy. "All these years. I never knew," he murmurs. No wonder his parents were protective of him. Over the years the protection must have become mutual, marriage unlikely, if not impossible, passion available only at the opera.

Light glints off the lenses of Sebastiano's glasses. "Now you know, *Professore*."

The waiter comes and asks if they want anything more. Both shake their heads. Anders reaches into his pocket and pulls out coins and paper Euros. The 2-Euro coins bear the famous profile, the fierce nose and jutting lower lip. "So Europe has crowned your poet with the laurel wreath, at least on its coinage," he says, smiling.

The concierge shrugs. "A bit late, don't you think, for a nod to Dante's fruitless desire to be recalled from exile to receive the poet's laurel wreath at the Battistero di San Giovanni?"

"Yes, a bit late," Anders admits. "But the Baptistery isn't far. Shall we pay a visit in his memory?"

Chapter Four

Leaving Gilli's, the two push through the throng along the Via Roma toward the old Baptistery. Anders feels caught up in the currents and eddies of humanity. Strangers brush by in their headlong way—Europeans or Americans, Japanese, Chinese—so many tourists with their mini-cams at the ready.

"Wasn't the Baptistery," Anders asks, "originally a sixth century temple dedicated to Mars?"

"Yes indeed" the concierge nods. "I suppose that to be baptized as a Christian in the former temple of the Roman god of war must seem ironic."

"Everything seems ironic to me these days, Sebastiano."

They haven't walked fifty meters before Anders finds he is staring at the back of the head of a woman in front of him. Something about her has caught his attention. In a minute, thoughts of the Baptistery vanish. He is staring at her so grippingly that his heart is pounding. A familiar ache of abandonment wrenches his stomach like a sickness. Is it possible? From behind, the shape of the ears, the chestnut hair piled up, those tortoise shell combs?

The same thing happened after Kate's death. After he'd been released from the hospital he had returned to the States with the children and stayed for a week with Kate's parents in New

York. Her parents had moved to Manhattan from Atlanta a year earlier, after Kate's father retired. Etched on the faces of his Southern in-laws during that month was their reproach that *he* had dared to survive, *his* hands on the wheel, while their daughter had died.

During that first week he had made excuses to leave the children with their grandparents to take afternoon walks in Central Park. He had looked up old friends and paced the streets, the act of moving his legs helping to take the edge off his desolation. During one of those Manhattan afternoons, walking east on West 57th Street, he had spotted, amid the bobbing heads in front of him, the unmistakable chestnut hair, the tortoise shell combs, and the gently scalloped shape of Kate's ears. Drawing nearly abreast of her, a choking lump forming in his throat, he'd called out, uncertainly, "Kate?" The woman had turned. The sight of her unfamiliar features had drained his blood.

It was not the only time during those Manhattan walks that the back of a head or contour of shoulders brought him up short. Once, he thought he recognized Mario, who owned the espresso bar, and Katerina, who owned the newsstand where he'd bought his *La Nazione* paper every morning. And Mauro the butcher, whose *macelleria* held the huge steel hooks hung with slabs of freshly slaughtered beef. It was as if some part of him was trying to use New York to forever imprint on his brain the town of Greve-in-Chianti, insisting that he never forget the year's life that he, Kate, Anna and Thomas had lived in Tuscany.

Anders slows his steps and falls behind Sebastiano. The dark-haired woman with the tortoise-shell combs, whoever she is, moves on with the crowd.

The concierge glances back. "Would you like to rest, *Professore?*"

44

"*Grazie.* I'm fine," Anders says, forcing a smile in spite of the heaviness inside his skull. "Can a man who smiles be in need of rest?"

"But what a smile, *Professore.*"

And it is true. Tears are rolling down his cheeks. He wipes them away and shakes his head. "Tears of joy. Now look," he says pointing ahead. "The oldest building in Florence, the Baptistery. It is Holy Saturday, the day of the week when babies were baptized. Maybe still are."

They go inside, out of the bright sun, and Anders' eyes adjust to the gloom. He gazes up at the mosaic that covers the west vault of the dome, where the figure of Christ is seated against a field of gold. Not far away squats a livid, horned Satan, his giant bat wings flared as his three serpentine heads sink their teeth into the naked bodies of sinners. Anders can't help recall the perverse eagerness of Dante's sinners, rushing toward their punishment.

Deep inside him whispers the voice of a young woman... *and you?*

Anders shakes it off. "What have I done that's so terrible?" he mutters. But a memory stays with him. He is in his Italian Medieval Literature class. Niven has taken a seat in the first row. She sits and scribbles her notes, occasionally glancing up at him with that cool stare of hers. At lecture's end she will rise and, before leaving, give him her enigmatic smile. Out of the corner of his eye he will watch her walk out the door, that tidy frame, her blonde French braid impudent in its perfection.

He had at first taken Niven for a teacher-pleaser, an achiever who would place great store in his opinion of her, giving him a chance at seduction. But he was soon undone by her emerald green eyes, and the slight smile that played about her full lips. He had underestimated her. Her *modus operandi* was not to

45

please but to conquer, to dismantle men to show they were nothing special. Not that he let on that she overwhelmed him. He bluffed that he had the upper hand—that as mentor he had firm control. If she spotted weakness, he was sure, she would lose interest and move on to new challenges.

He had been forty-nine and proud. Could his students have accused him of being a predator? His reputation as an admirer of young women may have preceded him, but to him he was simply a distinguished-looking professor who had developed a weakness for attractive young women since the death of the wife he had adored.

Looking up at the dome, Anders is mesmerized by the wax-yellow bodies of the naked male and female sinners agonizing there. After more than twenty-five years he can still hear the muffled thump that roused him from sleep that April night in his rented mountain cabin. There, lit by the flare of a Coleman lantern, Niven lay naked in a widening pool of blood on the bare pine floorboards. Grabbing her wrist, he felt only a weak pulse. In his horror he tried to wake her. His mind was losing traction. Where was the phone for an ambulance? For the police? But his getaway place had neither electricity nor a telephone. The cabin's attraction had been its romantic isolation. Panicked, he set the lantern on the floorboards and slipped his arms under her. His hands went wet with her blood. He mumbled: "Niven, for God's sakes, what's happened?"

Her lips worked, her eyes half open. "Terrible cramps." she whispered hoarsely. "I got up to turn the light on. Must have fallen. Need a doctor."

His sleep-fogged brain had grappled with the knowledge that the nearest medical help was more than an hour away, over rough roads. He wrapped her in the bed blanket and carried her, slipping and sliding in the blood she was still hemorrhaging, down the stone steps to his station wagon. He laid her out on the back seat—*laid her out*—that image of a corpse roosted in his brain as he hurtled down the mountain roads, praying that the doctors would save her.

At the hospital the ER medics in their green uniforms checked her pulse, put her on a gurney, and rolled her out of sight. Over an hour later a doctor appeared. "I'm sorry, sir, we gave your daughter plasma, and did everything we could, but she'd lost too much blood. I'm afraid we've lost her." He lowered his voice. "It was a spontaneous abortion, sir. Worst I've seen." He was a stocky, tow-headed young fellow, and he was shaking his head. Anders stared at him, trying to comprehend. They'd lost her? *He'd* lost her? Spontaneous abortion? She'd lost a child—*theirs*?

When he gave them his and Niven's names, and they realized he was not her father, their sympathy evaporated. They stared at him with disapproval. It was, after all, the Bible Belt. On the drive back, his mind replayed every second of every minute of the night before. He searched for clues by numb rote, as if the mystery of her death lay buried, waiting to be found. Had it been the bourbon's dulling sensation, keeping him hard deep inside her so long past the usual, she riding him, plunging toward some distant rapture, tearing loose the tiny child he'd known nothing of?

The newspapers carried the story the next morning. The female reporter chose to set the details against a backdrop of nationwide male predation. Writing the story, she would not have known of his helpless passion, wouldn't have known that their yearlong affair was ending. She would not have known that Niven was surely sensing the crumbling of his masterly pose, perhaps already sleeping with somebody else.

47

In the end the University, in spite of the rage of Niven's Savannah lawyer father, decided to keep him, creating a new status for a tenured professor: permanent probation, a kind of purgatory.

There in the Baptistery, Anders shudders. From high in the golden dome the baleful figure of Satan glares down at him. Andres turns away, shaking, to find Sebastiano staring at him, his eyes wide. *"Cosa c'è?"* the concierge asks. "What is it?"

It's my Niven, dead all these years, he wants to say. But he can only answer, *"Niente*—nothing." Anders takes a ragged breath and wanders away toward the baptismal font at the southeast side of the octagon. He must break the awful trance, search for a path away from thoughts of Niven.

Tourists have wandered into the Baptistery. Parents with children have clustered at a railing to view a dark, deep bowl on its marble pedestal. Staring at the bowl, Anders recalls visiting here with Kate and the children whenever they came to town. Each time, little Thomas would ask Anders to repeat the story about Dante saving the little boy. In the 1300s the baptismal font had multiple, water-filled ceramic tubes for simultaneous christenings. As the story went, a certain child, playing, had become wedged in one of the tubes, head down and drowning. Most of the onlookers were distracted as they watched a nearby baptism. Dante ran over and smashed the tube to save the boy. His political enemies later distorted his act, accusing him of sacrilege for smashing the sacred tube, ignoring his saving of the child.

"How did the little boy almost drown, Daddy?" Thomas used to ask, standing there in his Oshkosh B'Gosh overalls and navy sweater, his brown hair mussed, his blue eyes round.

"He was playing on the font and nobody even noticed when he became stuck."

"No one else was watching?"

"I'm afraid the priests were distracted by so many people and children. There were many baptisms on a Holy Saturday."

"Was the boy going to drown?"

"Yes, he was drowning. The tube was filled with water."

"And Dante saved the boy?"

"Yes, he broke the tube, so that the boy could be freed."

"Would *you* have saved the boy, Daddy?"

"Yes, of course," he would say, wondering if he would have.

And so it went, each time they visited. Anders himself pictured the scene as he told it to Thomas, the story of medieval Florentines unaware of an unfolding tragedy. Who would think of smashing the Holy Font to save a child?

And Anders? Why could he not have saved his little boy grown up, his Thomas, later when he needed him?

He loved his boy child. While Kate was buying clothes for Anna one morning, Anders took his three-year-old son up to see the church of San Miniato al Monte on its hill overlooking Florence. As they climbed the long flights of marble steps to the church, the sound of someone playing the organ came to them through the open doors above. They went inside. Thomas seemed transfixed by the notes of a Bach Fugue cascading through the vaulted space. He grabbed Anders by one finger and pulled him toward a bench to sit down. They sat and listened as Bach's music rolled over them. For Anders it felt as if his and his little son's souls touched.

In the end, years later, he failed Thomas. He never could penetrate the miasma that seemed to float up between them like a toxic fog, until they could no longer see or hear each other. There had been no momentous break, no storm of towering rage, only a slow distancing. Thomas's drug use began during his college years. Anders thought he noticed small valuables disappearing from around the house when his son came home for vacation. Busy as he was, he ignored it. He wrote off Thomas's seeming remoteness to the growing independence of all normal young people. There had been warnings from Anna about her brother's habits, but Anders had paid little attention.

Anders rubs his misting eyes and turns away from the font. What kind of man cannot save those he brought into this world? He throws a backward glance at the dome and at Satan. He feebly kicks at the marble floor with his bad foot and winces from the pain.

He turns to look for the face of Sebastiano among those gathered around the dark baptismal bowl. Instead, his eye catches that of a slender young woman with curly blonde hair standing apart from the others. She is wearing a yellow scarf, a beige cotton shirt with its tails out, and blue jeans. She is leaning forward at the waist as if to center the weight of her backpack over her hips. Most intriguing is the fact that he has just caught her staring at him. She looks away, pretending to study the bowl. Obviously a tourist, but is she English? French? He has found that young European women are more likely than Americans to find an older man worth glancing at. Something about the scarf suggests that she is French. He straightens up, works his face into a roguish expression and, trying to suppress his limp, strolls over to where she stands. *"Je vous en prie, mademoiselle...*the baptismal font is splendid, is it not?" he says in soothing French, his eyes fixed first on the bowl, then on her. She will intuit that it is she he considers beautiful, not the bowl.

She turns to him, her cheeks flushing. She says nothing. Her eyes are a crystalline blue, the color intensified by the reddening of her cheeks.

He is enchanted. "Is this your first visit to Florence?" he asks, again in French.

"Bitte?"

He smiles, embarrassed, and ransacks his brain for vestiges of his German. All he can dredge up are *"Fräulein,"* and *"Schlaf wohl,"* and those will get him nowhere. Stymied, his spirits sinking, he smiles sadly and bows. *"Auf wiedersehen, Fräulein."*

He limps out of the Baptistery into the sunshine. What could he have done with the girl, at his age? What in hell was he thinking? He spots Sebastiano standing nearby, elegant in his leather-buttoned cardigan and gray wool trousers. Did the concierge see him try and fail to pick up the girl? Anders walks over to him, prepared to make a joke of it.

Chapter Five

They have reached the Cathedral, the *Duomo*, with its marble bell tower, the *Campanile*, which with its hexagonal panels and carved lozenges, soars to the sky. Anders inhales the crisp autumn air, trying to raise his spirits after the deflating episode with the German girl.

"Sebastiano," he murmurs to the concierge. "What about the remarkable woman you're going to introduce me to? Who is she? When is that going to happen?"

"*Pazienza, Professore*. We will experience our evening diversion at her Palazzo San Giorgio very soon."

"I'm anxious to meet her," Anders grumbles.

It is noon, and the Via de' Cerretani is a maelstrom of traffic. Large orange ATAF buses lumber along, seemingly unconcerned at the possibility that they might squash one of the Smart cars or Vespas that dart around them like piglets around a mother sow. Anders' surroundings are so familiar that their reality is dizzying. Part of the vertigo is jet lag, part perhaps the stroke, but part also is the electrifying sense of having returned to this city, the emotional center of his universe, an amazed feeling of *can it be?*

Anders thinks back to the Florence of the early and mid '60s. *Motorini* mopeds were the main transportation for years after the war. The city was exciting, but not frenzied like the present.

He remembers strolling from the Stazione bus terminal to visit Kate at La Signora Rossi's for simple but elegant suppers. When La Signora wasn't serving dinner, he and Kate would search out a small *trattoria* and flirt over wine and pizza, or plates of pasta. Afterward they would cross the river to the Oltrarno district and devour *bongo-bongo* chocolate-covered ice cream puffs at their favorite *gelateria*.

He had been young, but astute enough to play up to La Signora, who after dinner allowed him a few minutes in Kate's room. He remembers Kate slipping out of her shoes, blouse, skirt and underwear in the cold room, her girlish small-breasted body shivering, barefoot as she was on the terra cotta tiles. He can see her jumping into bed and pulling the covers up to her nose, staring at him with her great brown eyes as he wrestled off his clothes. Making love had to be hasty yet careful, taking care not to make the bed squeak.

Anders notices that the concierge has been quiet. "What are you so deep in thought about, Sebastiano?" Anders asks, as they walk north on the Via de' Cerretani.

"I was just thinking of Dante's mentor, Brunetto Latini."

"Yes, a man of many talents. Why were you thinking of him?"

"Why? It was a case of the older man, attracted to his young protégé, using his elevated position," Sebastiano adds dryly, "to take advantage."

"You mean seduction? But homosexual love was fairly common in those days among the intelligentsia. In any case it seems the young poet rejected Brunetto's advances."

"For a while, perhaps."

Anders barely avoids a couple, walking arm in arm. "Well, we don't know the details, do we? But Dante made his old mentor pay the price—the Seventh Circle for eternity with the rest of the Sodomites."

"Yes, but when he came upon him there, in such sad circumstances, he pitied his old friend, as if he might run over and embrace him."

"Condemning him wasn't easy, was it? But he had no choice," Anders sighs. "His mentor's sin was a crime not against Man but against God. Brunetto had ignored Augustine's prescription for ridding the body of lust. Icy showers, the application of ice packs to the genitals, even binding and whippings—they were used for centuries to short-circuit lust, in obedience to the Church."

Sebastiano glances at Anders. "Augustine aside, is there not a certain precept that a mentor not take advantage of those placed in his trust?"

"Well, yes."

"It is not for me to say, but I remember one young student, among your *conquiste,* that you brought to La Lilia. I believe her name was Niven?"

Anders misses a step and is almost thrown off-balance. "Yes—what of her?"

"I recall your whispering that she was but one among several students you had taken under your wing. You were open about your conquests, a shock to me—sheltered as I was. My memory of your wife Kate was still fresh in my mind, seven years after her death on the *autostrada.*

Anders' throat catches. Is this concierge presuming to be his conscience? "Sebastiano, kindly do not discuss my beloved wife in the same sentence as my *conquiste,* as you put it. Seven years, by the way, is a long time."

"Forgive me, *Professore.* I forgot that time moves more slowly in America."

"What is this about, Sebastiano?" Anders snaps. "Seven years is a tenth of a Biblical *life,* for God's sake."

"An entire tenth, devoted to grief? *Dio mio.*" The concierge shakes his head. "Pardon me but I have known widows and widowers who consecrated twenty or thirty years—sometimes the remainder of their lives—to the memory of their beloveds. But maybe you consider such behavior self-indulgent?"

Anders tries to control his anger. He is on the verge of ending this little stroll. But he will not allow the concierge to ruin his first day in Florence. Not to mention the danger of continuing on alone with his balky right leg. Better to parry a thrust. "That's exactly correct," he snorts. "To make a display of grief for decades is gross self-indulgence."

"And so Dante's grief was mere self-indulgence?" Sebastiano says, his lips smiling but his eyes gone hard and bright.

"His wife outlived him," Anders says breezily.

"Yes, Gemma did. But Beatrice did not. Having crossed her path only a few times, barely exchanging greetings, he grieved for Beatrice the rest of his life."

Anders glares at the concierge. "I don't have to answer to you for the loves of my life. Besides, if Alighieri was so faithful, what about not only the Window Lady, but the mystery lady in Lucca? He even confesses his guilt by having Beatrice rake him over the coals in the *Purgatorio* for his faithlessness."

The concierge stops. "Faithlessness? You know that Beatrice was talking about Dante's falling by the wayside as a *Christian.*"

"And you know that it was not *just* Christian Faith that Beatrice was talking about." But standing there on the sidewalk, facing Sebastiano, jostled by passersby, Anders suddenly feels tired. The past that had flooded back and exhilarated him is now draining him. "So I loved, and mostly lost," he mutters, "but I've paid for my errors."

"And those who thought they had found shelter under your wing? Have they been paid?"

Anders explodes. "Who are *you* to accuse me? Are you so blameless? Keep walking, my good concierge, emblem of virtue," he blurts sarcastically.

Sebastiano gazes out over the throng crowding the sidewalk of the Via de' Cerretani. "So you protest, after so glibly explaining your seduction techniques while we sat over cappuccino at Gilli's? But I apologize, *Professore*," he says, giving Anders a thin smile. "Who am I to say such things to you? In any case, you will forget my lack of courtesy when you set eyes on the Contessa di San Giorgio. As a man who appreciates the fair sex, you will not be disappointed."

Now Anders is suspicious. What kind of woman does Sebastiano, in this strange mood of his, have up his sleeve? Is he gambling that Anders is hardly the man he once was with the ladies? Is this why he dares treat him with so little respect— old, sick and vulnerable as he is? Yet...yet. "Tell me again. Who is this woman, this Contessa?"

"You knew her many years ago, but time has passed. You would not recognize her."

"Her name again?"

"The Contessa di San Giorgio."

The name rings no bells for Anders. But why this introduction? In any case it is best to keep the peace. This concierge has the worldview of a cloistered clerk. He is an unlucky epileptic who has not lived a normal life. Sebastiano, he reminds himself, lives in an ideal world in which Beatrice's celestial garments are never soiled. He cannot understand that life has given a vital man such as himself opportunities that can force compromises. The fellow probably means well, walking ahead of him there, his head bent forward, dodging pedestrians left and right. But his experience has been severely limited.

"*Grazie, amico mio,*" Anders calls out, "for thinking to

introduce me to a new friend on this return of mine to Florence."

"*Non fa niente.*"

It's *nothing*? Not true, Anders thinks to himself, as he picks his way behind the concierge. There is much pleasure in the expectation of meeting an unknown lady—a Contessa at that.

There had once been another Contessa—a *Parisian* Countess. He had been in his early twenties, on his way from England to see Kate in Florence. He was in an *épicerie* in Paris, waiting in line to pay for a bottle of mineral water. Ahead of him was an attractive young woman buying shallots. He heard the female clerk say, "*Merci beaucoup, Comtesse,*" as she handed back her change. In seconds, after quickly paying the clerk for his mineral water, he was introducing himself to the young Countess, explaining in his schoolboy French that he was an American Francophile. His boldness and good looks won him her name, Marguerite, and the privilege of walking her to her car. He wouldn't let her open her Citroen's door until she agreed to meet him for dinner that evening. She was to pick the restaurant.

It turned out to be a very expensive restaurant, one that cost him many American Express checks. Fine wine had come from elegant taps at each table, and all three courses were exceptional. Giddy from the wine, they left the restaurant and walked along the Seine. "*Pardonnez-moi...*" she said after a few minutes, looking contrite. "*Peut-être c'était trop chère?*"

"Yes, expensive," he said. But it didn't matter—Marguerite was looking so lovely. With a boldness born of wine and a sense of little to lose, he swung her around and kissed her roughly, as if implying, *well, countess, I should get some appreciation for that fancy dinner, non?*

To his surprise she was completely acquiescent, seeming to

melt in his arms. He pulled her closer, and she sighed. He kissed her again, his hands roaming over her tender *derrière*.

He suggested they go to her place. No, her parents were there, she said, "but your hotel?" His wine-soaked brain had gone blank on his hotel's name—until ten minutes after they kissed good night.

Might Sebastiano's Contessa be as fascinating as Marguerite? She wouldn't be as young, of course. But there would be no question of parents getting in the way.

"And Professore," Sebastiano says, turning back to look at him, "speaking of those you sheltered, you did have children. Surely *they* found a safe place under your wing?"

Anders' thoughts of Marguerite evaporate. Had he ever taken the time to point the way for Anna or Thomas? Hadn't he been too busy chasing women?

Anders stiffens at what he has already acknowledged, nearly bumping into a couple of leather-jacketed Florentine youths walking abreast. Yes, he was a failure as a father, his sins those of omission. At the end of a stressful day Thomas might come up to him and ask him to throw a ball, or fix a broken toy. "Maybe tomorrow," Anders would say, or, "Haven't you got homework to do?" His son would blink and shuffle off to his room.

But why does he feel his stomach twist *now?* Why didn't he feel it *then*, this guilt? Anna, older, seemed more independent and self-contained. Less trouble. The experience of losing her mother seemed actually to have strengthened her. At least that is what Anders told himself. Yet Thomas seemed rudderless, and Anders could not relate to him, as if the interests of his son were those of a small, inscrutable alien.

Sebastiano has stopped in front of the Church of Santa Maria

Maggiore. The two of them stare at the massive stone edifice. The ancient façade with its great windowed diadem is not faced with the white and green marble of the Duomo, but with its original rough 11th century stone. The vertical windows are narrow and arched. Above the high peaked entrance is the statue of a saint. Anders has forgotten. Is it St. Bernard or St. Benedict?

"But why stop here, Sebastiano?"

"Latini's tomb is here. We were discussing him. I thought we might pay our respects."

"Not if it delays my meeting your Contessa. I know this old church well. What is there for me here?"

"It is a quiet place. I often come here to contemplate. Shall we, for a moment?"

Anders feels uneasy. He is not in a mood for tombs. But he shrugs. "If you insist."

They enter, and the vast space is almost empty. Two middle-aged women and an old man sit on benches several rows from the far altar. They are silent, bent in prayer. Anders and the concierge walk down the left aisle, their footsteps echoing from the vaults far above. The darkness reminds Anders of the Second Circle's gloomy cave where the shades of lovers Paolo and Francesca flew, circling in the dank air for eternity. *So true a lover*, murmured Francesca, *never to be parted from me...*

They stop in front of a small chapel to the left of the altar. Before it burn two thick candles, each set in a bas-relief-encrusted *candeliere*. A tall, yellowed column, blackened toward its top, stands at the inner wall of the chapel. There is an inscription on a tablet above the column but a railing prevents their moving close enough to read it. Anders knows it commemorates Latini, whose *Tesoretto*, an allegorical journey in common Italian—not Latin—so influenced Dante's work.

Anders shifts to his stronger left leg and inhales unseen air currents carrying the scent of incense and candle wax. "I always thought it strange," he whispers, "that the Catholic hierarchy honored Latini by burying him here in this old and revered church, given that Latini's sexuality was considered a sin against God."

Sebastiano shrugs. "The tomb was covered up at some point to hide the Church's error. It was only rediscovered during a renovation in 1751."

Anders stares at the small, darkened column. Latini died at age seventy-four. Dante was only twenty-nine at the time. He shivers as a mass of cold air from the upper vaults engulfs him. He pulls his heavy jacket tight. "What if Latini's love for the precocious young poet was so compelling," he whispers, "that he couldn't help himself? The poor old notary was perhaps sixty when he fell for Dante. Maybe he reined in his desire when the young man protested."

The concierge frowns. "To avoid repelling him? He knew Augustine's view, and Augustine was clear. Chastise the body."

"But when love has you in its power, especially if the love is hopeless," Anders murmurs, recalling Niven's glowing features. "Especially if the one you love, who you hope has feelings for you, turns away for whatever reason. That must have been difficult."

"I will take your word for it, *Professore*."

Anders glances at the concierge's profile, at the flinty gray eye staring at Latini's tomb. "Yet it was Francesca herself who lamented that Love pardons no beloved from loving in return."

Sebastiano clears his throat. "Over the centuries many died —some by their own hand, some by the hands of others—for loving a person forbidden to them. Adultery is a mortal sin and sodomites were thought possessed by demons. The Inquisition acted accordingly."

"Demons? Possession?" Anders recalls a museum exhibition he saw once in Milano. *Il Volto Peggiore dell'Uomo*— The Worst Face of Man. There, among the collected torture instruments used at one time by the Inquisition, were the Iron Maiden and The Rack. But there was also the Pyramid. A man or woman in heavy chains was made to sit naked upon the point of the Pyramid, the weighted body slowly forced down upon the sharp tip, driving it up through the anus into the abdomen, creating unimaginable pain and death. For homosexuals and prostitutes there was the Pear—thrust into the rectum or vagina, its razor-sharp leaves opened slowly by the turning of a screw, "exploding," in the words of the show's catalog, "the organ." Worst face of man, indeed. Unhappy lovers of either gender were lacerated, chastised, torn to pieces, as if the torment of unrequited love, the very thing that led the victim to transgress Church dictum, was not torture enough.

"You think that you are over passion's grip," Anders whispers to the concierge, "then back the fever comes. You can't sleep, can't eat, can't think."

"I understand, *Professore*," the concierge sighs, "but it would be no excuse. Brunetto Latini was a great man, yet in the end he was labeled a mortal sinner by even his beloved pupil. It was one of Dante's bitter judgments."

Anders surveys the chapel with its column and its burning candles. "And so how in the end does one calculate a mentor's responsibilities to his protégé?"

"The answer in ancient Rome was to instill the four virtues—Prudence, Courage, Temperance, and Justice. To those, the Christian era added Faith, Hope and Love. That would favor the protégé with the proper path."

"The proper path, with luck," Anders mutters. Turning toward the exit of Santa Maria Maggiore, he gazes at the vaults above him one last time. Might his and Kate's spirits some day circle through the smoky-dark air like paired doves, as Paolo and Francesca did?

Chapter Six

Leaving Santa Maria Maggiore, Anders and Sebastiano are carried along by the rush of people streaming east to the Duomo and the city center. Hungry, the two pause to admire thick salamis and pepperonis, cheeses and bottles of wine in the window of a *salumeria*. As they debate having salami or prosciutto sandwiches made up for them, a boy of about twelve emerges from the shop's doorway, pushing a battered red bicycle.

"...*e torna subito, capisci?*" shouts a short, plump, dark-haired woman following the boy, wearing an apron. "Come back right away," she says, shaking her hand, her fingers drawn to an emphatic point.

"*Sì, Mamma, sì,*" the boy shouts impatiently. He climbs onto his bicycle and begins pedaling up the Cerretani against traffic.

"*Stai attento!*"—"Be careful!" the mother yells, though her son is now out of earshot. She hurries back into the *salumeria,* shaking her head.

Anders points at the salami. "Really, Sebastiano, I wouldn't mind having her make up a couple of *panini*. We could sit and eat them somewhere. We're only a few blocks from the Duomo. Once, Kate, the children and I bought *panini* sandwiches at such a shop. We went to sit and eat them on Dante's *sasso*—the cast-off block of stone the poet once sat on to watch workmen lay the foundation of the Duomo."

Sebastiano wrinkles his face. "We are not *giovanotti* any longer, *Professore*. We have grown up. If you are hungry let us find a trattoria or even a pizzeria."

"I wasn't hungry until we came to this window and saw…"

But Anders stops. He has heard a distant metallic *thump*. They turn to look. Far up the Cerretani, cars and motorbikes are swerving and stopping. A man jumps out of his car and begins waving his arms in the air near what appear at this distance to be a bicycle and a small heap of discarded clothing lying in the street. The man approaches the heap, waving his arms, then turns to shout to the gathering crowd as if pleading his case.

The woman who moments earlier was scolding her son darts out of the *salumeria*. She is in tears, her face contorted with alarm. She hurries up the sidewalk, oblivious of others, wiping her hands on her apron, her short legs pumping in a rolling half sprint.

She was *already* in tears, Anders thinks to himself, stunned. *She knew.* How? She was inside her shop. "Did you see that, Sebastiano?"

"I saw it." The concierge's voice is flat, subdued.

"But she knew it was her *son* who had been hit." Anders' eyes follow the mother up the street. The gathered people make way for her as she reaches the driver, who has stopped and turned to face her. She disappears from sight as the crowd closes around them.

"She was busy inside the shop," Anders says. "She couldn't have heard the impact. It wasn't loud. How did she know?"

The concierge shakes his head. "The intuition of a mother?"

Anders steadies himself. "But it is, I don't know…supernatural. I saw it with my own eyes." He takes a deep breath. "No father would have sensed it."

"It would depend on the father."

Anders gives the concierge a swift glance. "No father would have detected it."

Sebastiano stares at him. "If you say so. I, of course, have no son. Still, I have not been insensible when those I loved were threatened."

"But did you have that mother's clairvoyance?"

"That shop lady was not seeing into the future, *Professore*. Her son was present to her, though he was not beside her." He studies Anders. "It must be a faculty which evolved over millions of years, don't you think? A primordial mother, searching for food for her offspring, away from her home, ever aware of their vulnerability whenever she left them alone?"

Anders is silent. He wonders exactly what he was doing when the overdose of heroin stopped Thomas's heart. Boiling eggs for breakfast? Waiting at the Volvo dealer for his car to be serviced? Parsing a Dante *terzina* for the class? Was there a slight flicker over the ESP airwaves that he never noticed? Did he mistake Thomas's brain going quiet for the onset of a mild headache? Had he been with Emily, the faculty wife he was bedding at the time? But he can't bear this train of thought. "I think I need a drink," he groans.

The concierge adjusts his glasses. "There is a little bar just south of the Duomo."

"Good."

Anders follows Sebastiano down the crowded Cerretani. Before they pass the Duomo they pass the scene of the boy's accident. As pedestrians jostle him, Anders can once more hear the mother's warning to her son: '...*e torna subito—and come back right away*!' What tricks is his mind playing on him? Years ago, Kate was practicing a Beethoven sonata for a recital in Greve's small concert hall. Mid-practice, she stopped and shouted, "Damn!" When he went in and asked her what the matter was, she said, "Oh, it's these *subito forti*." What, he asked, was a *subito forte*? "Literally, 'suddenly strong,'" she said. "A sudden spike in the music right in the middle of a hushed passage. Like a thunderbolt out of nowhere, a Beethoven specialty."

And that boy on the Cerretani, as he rode his bicycle, Anders realizes, he had his mother's *'e torna subito'* still ringing in his ears as the car came out of nowhere. For Kate, too, on the *autostrada*, a shattering crash out of nowhere. Why he is shaking? That at any moment the past can spike into the present?

Finally, some yards along the south wall of the Duomo he and Sebastiano pass the cathedral's black steel railing. There, behind the railing, is the ruined block of stone Dante sat on to watch the laying of the Duomo's foundation. Partially shaped by hammer and chisel on one side before being discarded, the rough gray stone appears out of place, forgotten, at the foot of the towering green and white marble casing of the Duomo's outer wall, as if nobody, centuries later, had thought to remove it once the construction had ended.

"Let's stop for a moment," Anders says, the years crowding him. "I need to rest. It's been years since I've been here, at this place, Dante's rock—his *sasso*."

The concierge steadies Anders as with painful care he squeezes himself under the railing. Lowering himself onto the ruined stone, Anders feels the warming heat of the midday sun's rays streaming down from overhead. He can almost hear the sharp cries of Anna and Thomas as they jostled for position on this very stone—along with Kate's commands to stop it. His mind flies back to an Easter Sunday, their first in Italy. Anna and Thomas had been begging for pets, a dog and a cat. Kate had approved, and so he had gone to Bianco Bianchi, the husky-voiced sixty-eight year-old *contadino,* a former farmer who tended a garden next to their rented farmhouse. Bianco used to ride a gearless old bicycle up the winding mountain road each day to water his vegetables. Where, Anders asked, could they find a dog and a cat for the *bambini?* Bianco rubbed his domed Tuscan forehead and thought it over.

That Easter Sunday Bianco appeared at the farmhouse in a shiny black Fiat driven by his son, Giulio. Father and son emerged from the car dressed in their white-collared, dark-suited Sunday best. There were greetings of *"Buona Pasqua"*—"Happy Easter"—all around. Out of the Fiat leapt a grace-ful dog resembling a black greyhound. For Anders it was as if an ancient shape had come to life straight off the wall of an Etruscan tomb in Cerveteri. His name was Argo, and he was a hound full of life.

Also in the Fiat crouched a black and white female cat. "Feed it bread," Bianco said, carrying it into the house. Kate mur-mured that cats don't eat bread. A few minutes later Bianco threw the cat a crust. Pinning it to the floor with one paw, the cat gnawed it ravenously. Anders and Kate were astounded. Before long, they had hens, then ducks. Anders took it on him-self to build a fence with a gate to keep the creatures from run-ning off. Consumed with his new barnyard, Anders was even forgetting about women.

"What are you thinking about, *Professore?* You look as if you might fall over."

Anders straightens and shakes his head. "I'm all at sea," he mutters. "I was thinking about the little family I had for too short a time. I find myself remembering things in the tiniest detail, things I haven't remembered in years. Like the faces of my *contadino* neighbor and his wife—she gave Kate the recipe for her *pommarola*—the tomato-based mix of onions, garlic, celery and anchovy simmered for over six hours. They were the ones who spotted little Thomas when he ran away one afternoon through the vineyard with Argo, our new dog. That was before I built a fence. I can see them as if they were standing before us right now."

The concierge gazes at him. "Yes, I have heard this from older friends. As the years pass, the earlier remembrances become freshest, and when death comes, one is deep in one's beginnings. It can provide an opportunity," he says, his voice softening, "for coming to terms with those *ricordi infelici*, those compromising memories of mid-life."

"Compromising?" Anders says, frowning. "I suppose. But I can see my little ones' upturned faces. I can hear Anna this instant as she points at the outside wall of this very Duomo, asking me 'Daddy, are the white and green stripes painted? No? Marble? How do they make the marble stick to the walls?' Another time I see her brooding face: 'Why didn't Dante try to marry Beatrice if he really loved her?'"

Anders turns to Sebastiano. "Do you understand what I mean?"

The concierge smiles, an upper gold incisor gleaming in the sun. "I believe I do, *Professore*."

Anders gazes down the length of the aisle that runs between the Duomo's wall and the railing. "Kate dead, Thomas dead, Anna grown up. All dead or gone."

Sebastiano stares up into the blue sky. "Losses. Dante had his. He was only seven when his mother died, and not quite nine when he met Beatrice Portinari, or 'Bice,' as her parents called her. His father died when he was a teenager. Death was a familiar companion in those times." The concierge shakes his head. "You have had tragedies, yes, but also joys. Your life has been like a movie," he says, turning his head away, "compared to mine."

Anders looks up, surprised. "Why do you say that?"

"The life of a concierge…" He stops. "Since childhood, when they had to remove me from the *scuola materna* and send me to special schools with the doctors, the medicines—'No, Sebastiano, you must do this…no, you mustn't do that. What if you have a *grand mal* seizure? Or even a *petit mal?*'" He jerks his head toward Anders. "I never had a family like yours to lose. Who would marry a man who isn't allowed to have a driver's license, a simple *patente*, because he might have a convulsion? Or a father who might collapse while carrying his baby daughter?"

Anders stares at the concierge. "It never occurred to me. But you have had a good job for many years now. You do it well, with, you know, a certain finesse."

"I have been lucky. The owner of the Hotel Lilia was my father's brother. My parents begged him to let me try working when I was young. In the beginning I cleaned floors for no pay. Then, when I didn't have fits every minute, my Uncle Federico let me stay. Only then did he begin to pay me."

Anders gazes at him and shakes his head.

"As for women, I am like our Dante, staring at his Beatrice on Sundays from four rows behind her. I worshipped *my* unattainable young lady like that every day of the week, imagining what it would be like to kiss such a girl, to hold her," he says, his voice dropping. "And then…" The concierge throws Anders a strange glance.

Anders' eyes flick away toward the tourists, the families, the priests, and the students strolling past them. Sebastiano's glance has made him shiver. *It can't be that the girl with the quicksilver eyes, his cousin…she could not have told him. He can't know, can he?*

"You see, *Professore*, from my remote vantage point you

have had a life the stuff of which artists use to create master-pieces. Verdi or Puccini could have created a dozen operas out of your life. But mine? Dante would have placed me in Hell's anteroom with those who lived without disgrace and without praise, with no proof to anyone that I ever existed."

"No, Sebastiano, that is too much," Anders says indignantly. "The anteroom was for those who could have chosen other-wise but didn't. Your choices were decided for you by your condition, your *malattia*. You're not being fair to yourself."

The concierge flashes a wicked smile. "But what if one uses such a thing as an excuse, to hide under a rock? What if I could have done certain things, but didn't?" His eyes glint. "I have free will. I *am* responsible. And I admit to being jealous of you, jealous of your wife, your children, the women you have had, jealous of the places where you have lived. I am most jealous of the sins in which you have indulged, especially the mortal ones."

The concierge's voice has a strangled quality. His normally pale, ascetic face is flushed and his chest heaves under his leather-buttoned beige cardigan. Anders is seized by the weird impression that Sebastiano is about to put his finger down his throat to make himself vomit.

"But you're not dead yet," Anders protests. "At your age you still have time for sinning, if that is what you want."

The concierge's face goes blank and his body seems to sag. "I have been whining nonsense to a man who is responsible and yet not responsible—a man unaware. Like certain criminals, who escape a prison sentence for reasons of insanity."

"You would accuse me?" Anders says, rising from the stone, trembling.

"As I said, you are not responsible." Sebastiano tilts his head vacantly, as if waking from a dream. "You must be hungry. If we take the Via del Calzaiuoli to the Via del Corso, to the heart of the old Sesto, where the Portinaris and the Alighieris lived, I know where there is a trattoria."

Anders grabs the steel railing. "Just don't torture an old man."

"You speak to me of torture?" the concierge murmurs.

But Anders hardly hears, his mind already elsewhere. He is responsible and yet not responsible? For exactly what, in Sebastiano's courtroom? Why does the concierge spring these charges? Why is today full of these *subito forti*—that bicycling boy, hit by that car? Why such reminders of Kate at her piano, of that last fight the night before the accident?

It happened on a day in April. He had driven up the winding road to the old farmhouse with its yellowed stucco that they'd rented a year earlier. He and Kate were lucky to have found it—originally one of thousands of crumbling stone *case colon-iche*—centuries-old tenant farmhouses that dotted the Italian landscape, abandoned as people moved off the land into the cities. This one had been renovated by the local Duke for rental on whose ancestral land it sat, less than an hour from Florence in the Chianti district.

That day, as he drove past two farmers—*contadini* trudg-ing back to town on the Chiantigiana at day's end after work in their vineyards—Anders had felt relaxed and pleased with life. He would be in time to bathe Thomas while Anna took her bath in the other bathroom. The children would have just finished watching their hour's ration of TV cartoons on RAI Due. Afterwards he would help Kate prepare dinner. She would have a *pommarola* simmering on the stove, the thick pasta sauce learned from Gabriela, the *contadino*'s wife. He would toss a salad, put out bowls for the children's yogurt, and set the table. It was a family routine that accommodated his research in Flor-ence as well as Kate's daily five hours of piano practice while the children were at school. As he drove up the twisting road he could make out their home. In the high distance it glowed a deep ochre under the setting sun. It would be a pleasant evening like any other in the past year, one he welcomed. He enjoyed being a householder, a father, as long as he could continue to feel like a man. And for that, he told himself as he parked the car, certain needs would occasionally have to be met.

Everything seemed as usual at dinner that night, except that Kate seemed preoccupied, sometimes not hearing the children's questions. She avoided his glances, even when clearing the dishes. After putting the children to bed upstairs he came down and found her sitting at the piano, bent over a piece of sheet music on her lap. He studied her for a moment— the figure of his wife in a pale blue sweater over a white blouse; strands of brown hair clinging to the collar of her blouse from static electricity. Thinking to brighten her mood, he took a silent step forward and put his hands on her shoulders.

"How did it go today?" he murmured.

"Why do you go wash up as soon as you walk in the door?" she asked quietly, without turning, as if addressing her sheet music.

Anders flinched at the brooding tension in her voice. "Why? Well, after a forty-five minute drive from the Biblioteca Nazionale Centrale, where I seem to spend half my life, I usually have a bit of a full bladder." He was trying to be offhand, even humorous, but he could feel her shoulder muscles stiffen.

"I asked why you *wash up* when you walk in the door. Not why you urinate."

"Kate, dear, my mummy and daddy trained me to wash after I urinate," he said lightly. "You know, cleanliness?"

She flashed him a wide-eyed glance. "You know I'm not talking about washing your hands."

His mind raced as he stared at the top of her head. They rarely called each other to account. It had been an unspoken agreement between them that two highly educated adults do not engage in domestic hysterics. Shrill confrontations were artifacts of the uneducated. But he knew what she was getting at. Yes, he had had occasional affairs, after a grace period of two years following their wedding. But from the beginning he had decided that sex on the side had nothing to do with Kate. His falling in love with stray women was beside the point. So why would he confess? Why rub her nose in the reality of his needs? He took a deep breath. "Now that you bring it up, I do tend to be a bit obsessive about cleanliness. Something about overly enthusiastic toilet training, I suppose."

She jumped up, whirling on him, spilling her sheet music onto the gleaming brown tiles. "Does your obsessive cleanliness explain why I received an anonymous phone call before you came home this afternoon," she said, her voice trembling, "some man insinuating in broken English that male dogs and husbands are known to wander?" Her head was shaking. "I don't think he was talking about Argo."

Anders' head spun. Who was the bastard? Nobody in Florence or Greve knew about the girl. He had been sure of it. Nobody at the hotel, unless she had said something—but she wouldn't have. She was too terrified of her father or her cousin finding out. He managed a shrug. "Kate, dear, Italians are devious. They are known for cooking up plots and trouble. Did it occur to you that some *dritto* in the area might have his sights set on you, and that his making me out to be a philanderer might give him the key to *you?*"

"Nice try," she said, glaring, her hands clenched. "And I don't buy the obsessive cleanliness ploy. Why should your urge to cleanliness become overwhelming exactly when you arrive home? I've never seen that need strike you when you've been *here* all day."

"Sometimes it does. But why are we arguing? I thought we decided long ago that squabbling was what other people did. Think now," he said, his tone persuasive, "if I've been home all day, not out and about, I don't *need* to clean up, do I?"

She stood, silent, tapping her foot. "You are a son of a bitch," she enunciated slowly and clearly. "Once, two months ago, the water line was out when you came home, and you couldn't wash. I could smell her, whoever she is, but I pretended to myself that I didn't, that it was an olfactory hallucination." She tilted her head back and smiled, her eyes mocking. "All I can say is, I'm glad I got mine."

Anders felt a shiver go up his spine. "What is that supposed to mean?"

"Meaning the horns on your head. I only regret the energy I've wasted on stupid guilt."

"What are you talking about?" he said, her words reverberating in his ears. He turned away. Did he really want to hear more? His eyes, for lack of anything better, fixed on the bars set in the casement windows. Italians, he thought irrelevantly, had always been fearful of thieves. The bars spoke of centuries of warfare and plunder, of desperate acts in desperate times.

"Thomas is yours. I made sure of that. But Anna? Have you ever wondered why she doesn't resemble you in the slightest?"

Anders felt dizzy. He was intensely aware of the after-dinner smells in the house: the lingering scent of the *pommarola* overlaying the cold fragrance of wall plaster, the pungent smell of tile wax. He hated the fact that the details of this moment would be imprinted on his memory for the rest of his life. "Who?" he whispered.

"A fling seven years ago," Kate said almost gaily. "David

74

was desperate to see me. I gave in, thinking that with all your adventures I could permit myself at least that."

"A fling you call it?" Anders shouted, feeling the rage welling up in his chest. "David? Wasn't he the one you…when I was in the Army in Korea?"

"The very one," she said solemnly. "He had never gotten over me, you see."

"And you knew, when Anna was born…"

"Actually, I didn't. At first I thought Anna was yours. I'd seen him just before you came home. I realized only later, as she grew older. It was her nose and her mouth. They're David's."

Anders felt a howl inside. There was no outlet for the rage. He was seized by an impulse to grab Kate by the throat, to twist and crush her white throat, to stop the breathing that fed the mocking smile.

"You want to kill me, don't you?" she said calmly. "Of course you do. I've done the one thing a husband can never forgive. Well? What's stopping you?"

He took two steps toward her. His eyes fastened again on her throat, that lovely lily throat sprouting from her pure white blouse. Behind that pretty face was the brain that had indelibly recorded in its neurons and synapses that last fuck with David, the bed they were on, the smell of his flesh…

"Well?"

"It's win-win for you, isn't it?" he heard himself say. "Killing you would put you out of your misery. And I would go to jail for life. And what about the children?" As he said this, his eyes went to the stairway. There, sitting hunched-up and small on the top step in her pink and blue nightgown, hugging her knees, was Anna.

Facing him, Kate did not see her. "Don't worry," she said. "We're in Italy. Here they only shrug at the murders of the

75

faithless Francescas of this world by outraged cuckolds. The worst you'll get is probation—like your probation at the university."

"Kate!" he said.

She followed Anders' eyes to Anna. "Oh, dear. Oh, my dear," she said, stumbling toward the stairway steps.

Chapter Seven

Anders and the concierge make their way from the Duomo, down the Via del Calzaiuoli, to the Via del Corso. Anders has been able to pull himself together after once again reliving the agony of Kate's revelation.

On the Corso they encounter two Asian girls walking arm in arm. "Tourists?" Anders asks Sebastiano.

"Probably two of the Chinese workers Florence has imported to help produce leather products," he replies. "The Chinese are hard workers."

The sight of their delicate round faces and almond eyes tugs at Anders' heart. So long ago, yet he can't forget that year in Korea. He had a girlfriend—*mamasans* the villagers called the troops' girlfriends—in the village of Tongduchon, just south of the DMZ. The girl's name was Miss Kim. There were many girls named 'Miss Kim', but this one was special.

"Sebastiano," he says, "I am no Catholic, and it's silly to ask, but..."

"Yes?"

"Man is punished for sin because free will allows him the choice to sin or not to. But what if some in hell are condemned for acts they didn't realize were immoral?"

"After God gave Moses the Ten Commandments there could be no excuse."

"True. But it also seems unjust that God knows a sinful act will happen *before it's even happened*. Can that be free will?"

Sebastiano gives Anders a sidelong glance. "Free will is not preempted, nor is responsibility for sin removed, simply because God knew of it beforehand. Aquinas was clear on that."

Anders' mind folds in on itself. Was Niven's death a consequence of a seduction he willed freely of his own accord? Did Kate's death result from an affair he willed, all his previous experience predicting such an outcome? Did his son die as a consequence of his father's willful choices in the years before his suicide? Was he, Anders, born to allow his son's death, God watching, knowing in advance that Anders Croft would *freely* choose the fatal choices leading up to that tragedy? But where was the justice in all that?

"*Professore*, are you all right?"

Anders is shaking. Sweat drips from his forehead. "Running sores, marks of Job," he mumbles, trying to camouflage guilt with wit.

The concierge sighs. "If you have them, *Professore,* they are invisible. But let us stop here and let me buy you something to drink." Sebastiano gestures at a small bar they are about to pass. "I think you need one."

Anders pauses, unsteady. "I'm still upset by the boy's accident on that bicycle."

Inside, they find themselves a table and order Campari. Anders studies a dark-haired young man standing at the bar. He is gulping *espresso*, this *giovanotto* whose ever-moving hands and jerks of the head remind Anders of a perky bird that has just alighted on a twig, ready to take off again.

"Are you becoming more comfortable?" asks the concierge.

"When I was in my early twenties," Anders says, as if he hasn't heard the question, "the Army assigned me to Korea as a medic with an infantry battalion not far from the thirty-eighth parallel. There were still traces of the war that had blasted the country into a wasteland. Outside our division compound was a mass of huts named Tongduchon. It had once been a traditional Korean village, but it had mushroomed as the people realized that performing menial services for the Americans would put rice and *kimchi* in their bowls. Korean 'boys'— grown men actually—shined officers' shoes and brass, cleaned their quarters, hauled garbage, sewed and repaired, did all sorts of jobs. A black market sprang up. Girls came from all over. The Koreans called them 'business girls.' Some were straightforward prostitutes, but others understood that a lonely G.I. boy, young and far from home, might be so captivated by the first love of his life that he might take her home with him when his tour ended."

"Camp followers," Sebastiano murmurs. "As old as war."

The waiter arrives with their glasses of bright red Campari and saucers of sliced blood orange. Anders takes a long draught of the bittersweet *aperitivo*.

"You were discussing Korean girls?" the concierge asks.

Anders sighs. "I was still in love with Kate. But after a while her letters trickled and stopped. I guess I became susceptible. For twenty dollars a month a soldier could set a girl up in a "hooch", as we called the village huts. That way we could have a regular girl when we were off duty. It was safer that way, too, with all the VD—if your *mamasan* stayed faithful. That was a big *if*. I saw plenty of gonorrhea cases in our battalion aid station, even second and third stage syphilis. Some of the infected troops avoided coming to see us, afraid they would get in trouble with the command. They knew we had to report such cases. So they would buy penicillin in the *'ville*," he says, using old G.I. lingo, "which often turned out to be Wildroot Cream Oil hair tonic. It looked like the real thing to a naive young private who injected it. The abscesses were awful. But I digress." He sips more Campari.

Sebastiano nods. "As a child after the war here I saw similar things."

"And so I found my Miss Kim, a name common in Korea." He circles the rim of his glass with his finger. "She was about five feet tall, with short black hair. An intense, expressive, little-girl face. She had a trim figure that made her look younger than she was. She told me she was a virgin. They all said that. Her English was fluent enough that I could translate some of Dante's *La Vita Nuova* into English for her. I told her the book is about Dante's inconsolable grief for Beatrice after she died, and the new life he then created for himself. The words seemed to hypnotize her. Perhaps she was pretending at first, but soon she began learning even the Italian. After a while she was memorizing whole cantos. By the end she was mastering the *Commedia's* intricate accents and meter. Miss Kim said I was such a good teacher, but she was the ideal student, bright and eager to learn compared even to my later university students."

"I suspect the poor lady had strong economic reasons to be motivated."

"I would not claim otherwise." Anders gulps more Campari. "Still, I found myself falling for her. After a while she began calling me Dante, and she wanted me to call her Beatrice, or just *Bice mia*. She worked out a few Italian recipes from a cookbook I found in the Post Exchange. She would take unfermented *kimchi* cabbage and ginseng and a few other Korean vegetables and make a tolerable Korean-Italian *ribollita*. Pasta was easy," he says, shrugging and smiling. "Weren't they making it before you Italians?"

"Possibly," the concierge says, adjusting his glasses on his nose. "And so you were obviously caught up with this young woman."

"When my tour ended, I initiated the paperwork for her immigration to the U.S. so we could marry. I went that far. Except that the Army knows how young solders' hearts can be captured so far from home. The paperwork slowed to a disapproving crawl, then stopped."

"So she was not able to follow you?"

Anders gazes out the window at the passersby on the Via del Corso. "Immigration restrictions. Her letters grew more frantic. Months passed."

"And that was the end of it?"

Anders leans back and smoothes imaginary wrinkles from his trousers. "I became obsessed with Kate again. I told myself Miss Kim would reclaim her virginity and find another G.I. as most of the girls did." He finds himself reaching into his shirt pocket for a nonexistent cigarette pack, all these years after quitting. "The hard thing is that eight months after I left Korea a parcel came. It was the copy of *La Vita Nuova* I had left with her. There was a letter from her parents, whom I had never met. They explained that my Miss Kim had thrown herself in front of a train. She had left her parents a note with my address, asking, *'Please be kind and return this book, Dante's* The New Life, *to Specialist E-4 Anders Croft, who must have found a new life himself.'* You see, once a woman became a business girl, she had no way back into traditional Korean society. She had to continue in the only role open to her—that of a G.I *mamasan.* Many such women, so isolated, eventually took their lives."

The concierge takes off his glasses and wipes the lenses with a handkerchief. "It is Puccini's *Madama Butterfly* again. May I ask how her death affected you?"

"Terrible guilt. When I think about it now, I feel that guilt again. But at the time, back in the States, I was obsessed with Kate's betrayal while I had been gone. She had taken up with someone else. I fought like hell to get her back. We finally got married. Six years later she betrayed me again." He shakes his head. "With the same man."

A long silence is punctuated by the chatter of customers standing at the bar. There is the clinking of glasses, the splash of cups and saucers being scrubbed in the small sink behind the counter. In the air is the faint smell of ammonia.

Anders has been staring out the window, occasionally shaking his head.

"We have had our *aperitivi*," the concierge finally says, "and now we must find a *trattoria* for our main course." He says it as if he is fulfilling a duty. "I happen to know of such a place."

Only a few of the dozen or so linen-covered tables of the brightly lit *trattoria* are filled when Anders and Sebastiano enter. The air carries the scent of grilled chicken, garlic, sage, and rosemary. A woman, fortyish in age, greets them in an odd outfit for a maitre d'—the studded, form-fitting black outfit of a bullfighter, her black hair pulled back tightly along her skull.

"*Buon giorno. Posso…?*" she asks.

Anders nods toward the tables. "*Una tavola, per favore.*

"*Benissimo.*"

She guides them to the back of the room to a table near a narrow Dutch door. The door's upper half is open, revealing a brightly lit, floor-to-ceiling glassed-in space. Inside, a ruddy-faced, heavy-set man in a white apron sits at a narrow counter beside a massive steel oven, pounding and kneading dough into saucer shapes. He raises a sweaty, bushy eyebrow at Anders and Sebastiano as they pass on their way to their table.

"Pizza-making as theater," Anders murmurs to the concierge.

The *torera* gives them their menus and leaves to fetch their requested wine, bread and mineral water. Scanning the menu, Sebastiano clears his throat. "Your Korean lover—it is a very sad story. Not to offend, *Professore,* but sometimes I cannot help wondering how it must make you feel to have helped Miss Kim, and Kate, and Niven—all these ladies—out of this world."

Anders, who is having trouble unrolling his napkin-wrapped silverware with his shaking left hand, gives Sebastiano a ferocious frown. "It was *not* my intent. I loved these women, you understand."

"As you loved what, *Professore?*' he says gently. "An exquisite painting? An endearing piece of statuary?"

"Passionately—I loved them passionately," Anders snaps hoarsely as he jerks his knife and fork free of his napkin. "Don't make me out to be heartless. You ignore my susceptibilities. And my bad luck."

"In medieval times men blamed their failings on being born under black stars. Do you believe you were born under black stars, *Professore?*"

Anders scowls at him. "Do I believe in black cats and witches, you may as well ask?"

"But you mention bad luck as a reason for your women's lost lives."

"Listen, I am not a rapist or a cradle-snatcher. I am not a criminal."

The concierge frowns. "Have I called you a criminal?"

"You *think* it." The words rise against a welter of imagined accusations, as if Kate herself were at the table, staring at him. "Sebastiano, I've wondered about something all these years. I've wondered exactly who telephoned Kate about my affair with..." he begins. *But what if the concierge really does not know? The man's own cousin...*

"Excuse me?" Sebastiano looks mystified. Except that there is a tiny sparkle in his eye. "You are speaking of one of your affairs?"

"I am speaking of a bastard *dritto*," Anders says, glaring, "who telephoned my wife one day thirty years ago, slipping a viper into our marriage by accusing me of infidelity. The next day I was crazy and exhausted from a sleepless night of our fighting. I made a bad decision on the *autostrada*. She died."

"A bad decision," the concierge murmurs gravely. "I admired and respected your wife. For me her death was tragic." He pauses before beginning to inspect his menu.

At a loss how to respond, Anders allows his eyes to roam over the entries on his menu: *bruschette* with white beans and new olive oil; chopped anchovy and chicken liver on small *crostini* toasts; *penne* pasta with swordfish and eggplant in olive oil; ribbons of *tagliatelle* pasta with mushrooms; *ravioli al pomodoro*. But now he has no appetite. The concierge, with his insinuations of his criminality, has stifled it.

"*Pronti?*" A young dark-haired waiter has appeared, all business. "But you're not ready—shall I return?"

"Wait," the concierge says, glancing at Anders. "I am ready. For me, a simple *ribollita*."

"For me the *tagliatelle*," Anders mutters. But he brightens. "Are there still any fresh figs to be had?" Anders visualizes the tall fig tree that stood outside the farmhouse in Greve. In early September he and Kate and the children would pick them when they were soft and green.

"*Ma non, mi dispiace,* the season is over. But we have apples, pears, bananas, even dates."

"Then just *vin santo* afterwards, with *biscotti*."

"*Certo.*"

Anders notices half a dozen girls, perhaps fifteen or sixteen years old, entering the restaurant. They hesitate. A waiter rushes up and offers them a long table parallel to the front window near the door. As they seat themselves, Anders notices one in particular. She has shoulder-length blonde hair, perhaps not washed today, since it hangs in strips. It's a look he prefers to the usual sheaf of yellow wheat. He watches her choose a chair at the end of the table closest to the door.

The concierge is tapping the table with his fingernail. "*Professore,* I sometimes forget that your middle name is Jason. It makes me think of the Jason of Greek myth—and the regret of the women who became entangled with him."

"What's this?" Anders snaps, his attention to the girl interrupted. "What Greek myths?"

"Sometimes they speak truth, *amico mio.* Think of Jason and his Argonauts, shipwrecked as they were for two years on the island of Lemnos. Think of how he and Hypsipyle, the island's queen, fell in love with each other. Think of how badly it ended for her."

"It seems it always does," Anders mutters.

"The Lemnite women forgot to sacrifice to Venus, and the angry goddess made them hideous to their husbands. The husbands avoided them and their scorned wives killed them. By the time Jason arrived, there were no men left on Lemnos."

"Serves the women right," Anders growls.

"So imagine what a figure the ship-wrecked Jason must have presented, all tanned and muscled from weeks at sea. Can you imagine how he must have looked to the poor, man-starved Queen of Lemnos?"

"Quite a sight, I'm sure," Anders says, "but she shouldn't have killed her husband." He has been keeping his eyes on the girl, fascinated. He can see only her right side in profile. She has on jeans and an open navy blue parka shell. As he watches, she takes off the parka shell and turns to slip it onto her chair back, revealing her girlish figure in an olive cable-knit sweater. At the distance of about fifteen feet in the brightly-lit room he can make out the wool cables running lengthwise up her sleeve to her shoulder, meeting, at ninety degrees, the cables that have run up her back, over her shoulder and down her front, over her maidenly breasts. He guesses that she probably stands five and a half feet tall. Her complexion is light for an Italian. Even at this distance, as he catches bits of their chatter, he can pick out her low, excited tones and distinguish them from the sharper tones of the others.

"No, she shouldn't have," the concierge replies, "but neither should she have trusted Jason, a rake as anyone could see."

The young dark-haired waiter reappears and sets a bottle of mineral water and a basket of heavy-crusted Tuscan bread on the table. He ceremoniously fills their wine glasses, gives them a quizzical glance, and departs.

"Rakes, doing their raking, are one of the reasons we have babies," Anders says, reaching for his wineglass. He savors the earthy, robust taste of the Chianti. "As I remember, the gods kept storms around Lemnos for two years. The Argonauts couldn't leave the island until the gods let them. Jason finally set sail to find the Golden Fleece."

"In doing so, he abandoned Hypsipile the Queen."

"Couldn't be helped." Again Anders gazes across the room. The girl's profile—her classic brow, nose and chin—reminds Anders of an ivory cameo. Twice now she has glanced in his direction, possibly at the nearby pizza man. Anders can see him out of the corner of his eye, stretching and broadening the dough into flying saucer shapes. Or could the girl be looking at *him,* a professor past his prime, whose glance may yet carry some of its old charm? The possibility is slight, but in truth he would rather she not notice him. Aware of his stare, she might become self-conscious, like a surprised doe. She might blush, and become nervous. Alighieri would have understood, discreetly watching his delicate Beatrice during Mass from several rows behind her.

Sebastiano clears his throat. "Before Jason sailed away, *Professore*, Hypsipyle asked him about her two sons, ones that he had fathered. Was he abandoning them, too?"

"Sons!" Anders muses aloud. "Was it his fault the gods' storms kept them on Lemnos for two whole years?" His eyes follow every movement of the girl's head, every tiny shift in the planes of her profile, the movement of her lips as she confides a word or two to her friend sitting to her right. "Quite some storms," he mutters, "to last two years, don't you think?" The girl glances in his direction again—perhaps toward the pizza man—but this time turning her head, giving him a split-second view of her full face. Her cheekbones are wider than he expected; she looks exotic, almost Slavic. The difference between the frontal and profile views gives the impression of two girls in one. But the eyes! Something about her eyes, and the shape of her face, even from a distance of fifteen feet. He adores her already.

Sebastiano chuckles. "The gods could do anything, *Professore*. A two-year storm was child's play. The real question is why Jason's love for his Queen lasted no longer than that."

"You'd have to ask him," Anders says, agitated.

"Poets had varying versions of the myth," the concierge continues. "Ovid's version was that Jason abandoned Hypsipyle before the second of his two sons' birth. Statius wrote that Jason had only one son, born before he left Lemnos. Dante decided in favor of Ovid. And you, *Professore*?" The concierge pauses. "Which do *you* prefer?"

"Which do *I* prefer?" Anders answers, startled out of his trance. How did Sebastiano catch on to his voyeurism, all the while droning on about the Argonauts? "I suppose if I were sixteen," he mutters, "I would choose the one on the end, with the olive sweater." He glances at the concierge. "But I am no longer sixteen."

Sebastiano's expression remains one of quiet amusement. "No, you certainly are not. And here I was comparing Ovid and Statius. But your taste is fine, as always," he says, nodding in the girl's direction. "I'm sure you would make her a fine grandfather."

Riveted by the girl, Andres barely hears the concierge. Maidenly, he thinks—that's it. She is so *maidenly*. That word alone sends him back decades, again to the young Eleanor, filling him with a hopelessness he has not felt for years. Even if he could talk to this girl, even if he were fifty or sixty years younger, what could he say to her? She would give him a careless glance, the corners of her lips turning up in polite bewilderment, or worse, amusement. Even if she did respond, no matter what lengths he went to, no matter how much charm he exerted, he would never be able to possess her. Not a half century ago, not now, not ever. She would say something girlish, or sly in a naïve sort of way, surprised at his sudden attention. But she would be unavailable. He feels the abyss. He and she exist in different worlds. It's a strange lurch into despair he feels, but he can't take his eyes off her. As other people enter and are shown tables, he is gratified that none block his precious line of sight.

After half an hour they are eating the last of their food and drinking the last of their wine. The room has almost filled. Anders knows he doesn't have much time left. His line of sight to the girl still exists, but only if he leans slightly to his right.

It is a shaft of imagined possibility. She and her friends have finished their pizzas. He tries to press the image of her face into his brain. What *is* it about her face, her eyes?

Sebastiano carefully wipes his lips with his napkin. "Dante's verdict, of course, was to condemn Jason to the Eighth Circle with the rest of the gang of Seducers. Demons whipped the kingly seafarer as if he were nothing but a lowly slave." He pauses. "Yet Dante's Jason shed no tears. Do you think it was because he was unrepentant? Or was he too kingly? Which would you guess, *Professore?*"

"What?" Anders tries to grasp the question as a party of four fills the precious sliver of space, obliterating the girl at last. "What in hell are you talking about, Sebastiano?"

"In Hell, exactly, *Professore.* Our magnificent Don Juan, as one scholar put it, covered with shame."

The girls are getting up. Anders can now see them again, talking and laughing. *She* pulls on her navy blue parka shell and whispers a comment to her friend. Now she turns in his direction and seems to smile—is it possible? At *him?* Anders is flustered. He does not know whether to smile (stupidly) or whether to maintain a discreet, dignified pose. Yes, she *is* making her way toward their table. He can see her eyes clearly now—eyes of luminous gray, almost liquid silver. Only once in his life has he seen—it is not possible.

The girl walks straight up to Sebastiano, leans over and confides something to him. As if in afterthought she gives Anders the briefest smile.

"Pamphila," the concierge says to her, "may I introduce an old friend, *Professore* Anders Jason Croft."

"*Piacere,*" she says, softly, her brilliant eyes lingering on Anders for a moment, before she turns and leaves.

Anders, near paralysis, watches her glide past the intervening tables to rejoin her friends waiting at the door. The angel—*she spoke to him.*

"*Piacere,* she said," Anders murmurs. "A pleasure."

The concierge cocks his head at Anders. "How is your state of mind, *Professore?*"

"Who *is* she?" Anders whispers hoarsely.

"She is the daughter of the Contessa di San Giorgio, the lady we will soon be visiting. Pamphila is fortunate to have inherited her mother's remarkable eyes."

Chapter Eight

"Sebastiano," Anders says as they leave the *trattoria*, "I have seen only one woman in my life with eyes like that, and I will never forget her as long as I live."

"Now there may be two such women."

"I can't believe it! The Contessa we're going to visit—she's my little Diana? That was really her daughter we just saw?" Anders demands, still flustered. His world feels skewed by the slipperiness of time. "What am I supposed to say to her after all these years?"

The corners of Sebastiano's mouth curl into a smile. "You will say '*Che gran piacere, Contessa*—What a great pleasure!'"

Anders tries to picture the Diana he knew, that slip of a girl with her ash blonde hair and Botticelli features, a girl seemingly credulous, seductive yet serious, a mysterious light shining always from those silvery eyes. At sixteen, she seemed far older than her years, as if his offer to teach her English—and other things—had come none too soon. Now she is a Florentine noblewoman, surely a gracious yet formal aristocrat who will smile with restraint at memories of the old days and move on to a more comfortable topic. But why has she asked Sebastiano to bring him to her? What does she want? He feels a warning queasiness in his stomach—that vague sense of guilt he used to feel when running into an ex-lover he may have wronged.

His mind slips back decades. After the accident, Diana had visited him at the hospital. The first day she brought him tiny raspberry and blueberry *torte* from Giacosa. He couldn't eat them because his lower jaw, shattered by the steering wheel, was wired shut around the tubes that fed him, but he was grateful for her attention. As for speech, he could only grunt. There she stood by his hospital bed, the Giacosa box in her hands, staring at him. Her liquid-silver eyes were moist with something between pity and horror. *"È tutta colpa mia…"* she said over and over that first day. He did not understand what she meant: how could it have been her fault? What could she have done? He remembered only that they had had torrid sex the day before the accident, parked in the hills north of the city, he sitting in the passenger seat of his four-door Alfa, she facing him on his lap with her skirt pulled up, her bare knees clenching his bare hips, squirming down on him.

Diana had visited him in the hospital twice more. He hadn't been able to touch her soft hand without flash visions of blood and smashed glass, mangled limbs and twisted metal that some part of his imagination seemed to have collected and preserved. Why? Was it her *"…colpa mia?"* No, he soon realized, it had to be from the trauma of having glimpsed Kate's smashed and inert body beside him in the car.

Diana appeared to sense this, becoming more self-conscious with each visit. Their habit of teasing each other, grown out of their original flirtation, had disappeared. Her last visit came three weeks before he was released. "But how could this happen?" she murmured as if to a higher power with whom there had been a secret compact, now broken. By the end of her last visit he felt her giving up on him—on them—giving up on what had connected them. Or was it *he* who gave up, besieged by shock and guilt at Kate's death?

Sebastiano had also visited the hospital, giving him updates on how Anna and Thomas were faring with the housekeeper. The concierge had gazed at him gravely, something unspoken hanging in the air.

Gradually, the memory of Diana and their trysts passed as if into a black hole, along with the accident and everything else from that time. Except that her shining eyes would appear at the strangest moments over the following decades, accompanied by an echo of her voice whispering of feelings he had himself once known in his youth.

As Anders and the concierge leave the old *Sesto*, the neighborhood of the Portinari and the Alighieri, the sky seems to be darkening from the east. They hear a distant rumble as they pass the long Banca Toscana building that occupies the site that Beatrice Portinari's house occupied seven centuries earlier. They turn down the Via Santa Margherita and pause in front of a tiny restored church near the site of the original Chiesa di Santa Margherita, long since demolished, where Dante had gazed at the oblique profile of his Beatrice at Mass every Sunday morning.

"Tell me about Diana," Anders says, "about her life since I last saw her."

The concierge shrugs. "After you left Italy she turned to friends her own age. A year or two later she became involved with a fiery young man of the Left, as so many were in those days. She dropped out of sight into the underground for a while. Perhaps joining *La Sinistra* was part of her ongoing war against her father, a man too involved in his business dealings and love affairs to see that he had a daughter. Of course it may have had to do with the residual influence of a certain departed mentor."

Listening to the concierge, Anders once again imagines the

sweet girl whose magic had come so close to warming a cold corner of his heart. Beatrice must have had such eyes—eyes the poet wrote, that glowed with a holy light.

In their early days together, he sometimes caught Diana staring at him, as if wondering something. Exactly what, he never understood. But he took it as a convenient cue to speak English, to teach her a few words, to put things back on track, since it was within the teacher-pupil relationship that they kept meeting in the Biblioteca, in cafes, on the street, in his car. He never troubled to ask about those probing looks any more than he asked himself why a married man with two children was having an affair with a teenager. He accepted them as signs of a young girl asking herself why a wise and experienced professor would take an interest in her, even as he slipped his hand around the waist of her clean and neatly pressed school uniform. Was Diana looking for a father? That idea fills him now with something queer and unfamiliar, something approaching shame. He shivers, as if a door long closed is pried open a crack: has it something to do with the loving father he has never been to Anna?

"La Contessa di San Giorgio is a quite different person now," Sebastiano says with fresh energy. "She is sophisticated, an aristocrat, whether she married into it or not. She learned quickly. In many ways she is more the Contessa than her husband is the Conte. And she is a good mother. Yet beneath the veneer there still are flashes now and then of the lively young girl."

"What is the Count like?"

"The Conte di San Giorgio? In this day and age a member of the titled nobility has the option of being eccentric, even humorously *buffo*. The Count carries his title lightly. He and she have developed an arrangement over the years that allows each considerable liberty. He is more accommodating to her than her father was to her mother. He also respects the funds her family provides for the upkeep of the Palazzo San Giorgio. You will notice that they have a deep and sincere affection for each other."

A twinge of jealousy jabs at Anders. "I see," he says. "A marriage in the fine old European tradition. New money re-invigorating diminished old money."

"But successful only when both sides are content." Sebastiano adjusts his glasses on the sharp ridge of his nose as he gives the sky a wary glance. "And now we must hurry to her home, only a hundred or so meters from the Piazza dei Cavalleggeri." He tilts his head at Anders. "I believe you know the area—on the Lungarno della Zecca Vecchia."

Anders examines the concierge out of the corner of his eye. Could Sebastiano know that the Biblioteca Nazionale was the usual jumping-off place for his and Diana's trysts? There were afternoons, after lunch, when they would meet in the stacks of the Biblioteca, rush out of the building, cross the Piazza dei Cavalleggeri, and hurry over the Ponte alle Grazie, bursting with anticipation, to his car?

"I see by your expression that you remember the Biblioteca," the concierge says with a hitch in his stride, as they walk toward the Via Proconsolo.

Anders stares at the concierge's back. "Sebastiano, I don't understand. You have watched Diana's love life, watched her put what I assume was a smile on her absentee father's face as she made an excellent marriage. You watched her belly grow with the Count's child." He shakes his head. "Heartbroken, even as a cousin, how could you bear to remain in Florence?"

"Where would I go?" The concierge laughs bitterly. "Even Dante, after Beatrice married, stayed in the city she made sacred for him so that he could be near her. It is much of the reason his exile was so painful. He never forgot her. Quite the opposite. You must understand, I am only a witness to Diana's loves. As when I go to the opera, to listen and to watch. When I am alone I sing the arias badly, careful that no one will hear. That is all." The sky rumbles and he checks his watch. "*Professore*, we must walk quickly. The storm is coming and we have only fifteen minutes to reach the Palazzo San Giorgio. I would rather not be late, arriving soaking wet. There will be time for talking when we arrive, believe me."

At that instant the heavens explode in a blinding flash and clap of thunder. A cable, hung from an overhead roof, sways and disintegrates along its length, raining fiery sparks down on them. "*Attenzione!*" Anders yells, tripping as he tries to avoid the shower of fire.

"*Dio mio,*" shouts Sebastiano, as he scrambles out of the way. Moments later, his face pinched and pale, he is helping Anders to his feet. "But look at you, *Professore*. Your eyes are bulging as if you saw Satan himself."

"I nearly did!" Anders mutters. "That was close." His heart is pounding. The smell of ozone is overpowering. It jogs the memory of a lightning strike thirty years in the past. On a hot July afternoon he had driven Diana up to the Prato Magno, the high mountain meadow east of the woodlands of the Casentino, where fragrant lavender grew wild underfoot. Standing on a knoll in a world of their own, they gazed across the valley, inhaling the lavender's scent, as they listened to the dull *clunk* of cowbells far below. He gradually became aware of a faint crackling sound, like that of crumpling paper. He assumed it to be some sort of altitude effect. The crackling grew louder, and only when he felt his hair standing on end did he turn to see a huge black cloud rushing toward them from the direction of the Casentino. He grabbed Diana's hand, and they ran in terror. Seconds later, lightning struck the high ground they had just left.

He would never forget the thick, hormonal scent of the ozone. "We almost became like Paolo and Francesca," Diana cried, her eyes luminous and round as she evoked the adulterous lovers. They ran to the car and made ferocious love as rain hammered the Alfa's steel roof.

"We are late!" the concierge barks. "Come, hurry, Professore—we have a few turns before we reach the river." As raindrops fall, Anders hobbles after the concierge, through the piazza and onto the Lungarno, the walk that edges the river. Black clouds boil down from the east amid flashes of lightning. Gusts of rain sweep the river's surface.

Suddenly they find themselves standing before a massive three-story palazzo. Anders is surprised by its resemblance to the Florentine Palazzo Grifoni with its tall glowering windows, its projecting corbels, and its façade of sculptured motifs in the Mannerist style.

"The brick frontage, such a Roman influence," Anders remarks. "So unusual in Florence. Why haven't I noticed this building before? I thought I knew this area."

"Perhaps you were distracted by other matters," the concierge answers dryly, as he rings a bell beside the massive oak doors. "But you would not have missed it when it was built, late in the sixteenth century, standing solitary and grand with its geometric gardens. As the city expanded, the gardens disappeared. At least there remained the view of the river, which you could watch from the majestic *inginocchiate* windows that reach almost to the floor. Palazzo San Giorgio is an artifact of a different age. Yet the Conte and Contessa make it their comfortable home—one in which the fifteenth Conte of San Giorgio and Diana have raised their daughter, Pamphila."

Anders recalls that *inginocchiate* windows, so low, imply a kneeling in prayer before the Cross. He turns toward the river and brushes stray hairs out of his eyes. It is always miraculous for him that the surging Arno he sees today is the same river Dante and Beatrice knew—the same one whose bridge he and Diana ran across, years ago. "But Sebastiano, answer me. Why would Diana want to see me again after all these years?"

The rain is beginning to fall and the concierge is ringing the bell again.

"Why?" he asks. "All I can say is that when I happened to mention that after many years you would be visiting our city again, she insisted that I invite you. You may not see the Count, preoccupied with his various interests. He set up living quarters some time ago on the ground floor while she remains above, on the second floor, the *piano nobile*." After smoothing his trousers, Sebastiano's fingers fly over his cardigan's buttons to be sure they are fastened. "I think I hear footsteps."

The left of the two tall doors opens. An older man of medium height and slight build appears and bows, his eyes fixed on the wide stone threshold. He is dressed in a forest-green uniform with golden epaulets, maroon suede collar and lapels, and matching green cap with shining black visor.

"*Filippo, buona sera,*" Sebastiano says, nodding politely.

Anders senses that the concierge is about to add a comment but resists. Is it about the gaudy uniform? But Filippo steps aside and solemnly motions for them to enter.

Inside, Anders' eyes slowly adjust to the semidarkness of the palace interior. He notes white fluted pilasters set into slate-gray walls. A dozen steps further, he finds himself in a spacious central atrium. High overhead are the arches of huge barrel vaults. Galleries march off to the left and to the right. Straight ahead across the marble floor begin two flights of stone stairs that curve symmetrically away, then toward each other, rising to the top at what Anders assumes is the *piano nobile*. Above the double staircase hangs a massive unlit crystal chandelier.

As he turns toward Sebastiano to comment, Anders notices a figure seated in the next gallery. A man in a violet-colored smoking jacket is seated in a large armchair, a cigarette holder in one hand. He is leaning down to stroke a small brown and white dog. The man glances toward them and raises his eyebrows, as if suddenly aware that guests have arrived. The dog stares at his master with such stark stillness—apparently begging—that it almost appears stuffed.

"That is Cangrande," Sebastiano says with a twinkle in his eye. He takes off his glasses and wipes raindrops from its lenses with his handkerchief.

"*What's* his name?" Anders whispers.

"The dog's name." The concierge gives Anders a sidelong smile. "It's a play on the name of the Veronese nobleman, Cangrande, who hosted Dante during part of the poet's exile. The name translates as Great Dog, in English. It's a funny name for a little terrier—an example of the Count's sense of humor."

"Of course I knew about Cangrande della Scala. I just thought you were talking about the Count."

"I know," Sebastiano says, chuckling. "And you thought that *was* the Count."

"What?" Anders exclaims.

"*Volete salire?*" Filippo breaks in, bowing and gesturing toward the twin staircases. "The Contessa awaits us above."

"*Grazie, Filippo*," the concierge murmurs.

Taking his steps carefully as he ascends, Anders notes that the chandelier's crystal is so dusty that the sparkle is gone. Holding onto the thick stone balustrade to steady himself, he peers far up into the shadows at the point where the chandelier's cable is attached to the ceiling.

"The pulley which allows me to lower and clean the

candeliere, is out of order," Filippo says, as if reading Anders' mind. "Otherwise I assure you the crystal would be polished."

Anders is struck not only by Filippo's fastidiousness, but by a certain gentility in his speech. He must be a faithful retainer, he gathers, trained in the old ways to anticipate the lord's every wish, including the regular polishing of hundreds of the chandelier's crystal bits and pieces, experiencing a sharp sense of failure when circumstances deter him from his work.

By the time they reach the top of the stairway, Anders pauses to catch his breath. He notes a change in the decorative scheme. An ornate frieze in a Greek Key design runs around the tops of the walls above a creamy trompe l'oeil bas-relief of tiny classical figures. Except for a half dozen Savonarola chairs ranged along the walls, their curved wood splines dark with age, this *piano nobile* room is empty. Whereas the ground floor was marble, here the floor is laid out in a parquet of light and dark wood in geometric designs. From where they stand, galleries stretch off to the right and to the left, like those of the floor below. Quite a way of life, Anders reflects.

"Per piacere," Filippo says as he leads them into the next room, similarly vast, with a nearly thirty-foot ceiling, its walls covered with maroon brocade.

Anders gazes up at the frieze with its interlocking Indian swastika figures. Its gilt is brighter and its stucco cleaner than on the lower floor. Covering the ceiling, framed by the frieze, are scenes painted in *fresco* in delicate greens, reds and blues. From the occasional chipping and peeling, Anders can see that they have stood the test of centuries. Evenly spaced in the wall facing the river are four of the *inginocchiate* windows. They flank a broad fireplace whose flue rises, gradually flattening and disappearing, into the upper surface of the brocaded wall.

Set before the fireplace is an elegant couch covered with a

faded, ivory-colored fabric matching that of the window curtains. A low *pietra dura* table sits before the couch, its surface a brightly colored mosaic of tiny colored stones. A crystal ashtray seems almost a part of the mosaic. Arranged around the table are four leather-seated chairs with high, carved-wood backs.

Filippo nods toward these. "Please, make yourselves comfortable—the Contessa will be here shortly." He leaves, and Anders hears his footsteps descend the stairs.

Anders and Sebastiano seat themselves and glance around the room. All is quiet, except for the wind rushing against the windows as the storm outside surges down the river. Anders is too wary and unsettled to expect a tender meeting with a long-out-of-touch girlfriend, even if *he* has sweet memories of the old days. He might as well be sitting in the waiting room of a neurologist to diagnose the seriousness of his latest stroke. It is time to quell his anxiety with a joke. Anders clears his throat.

"Sebastiano, do you suppose Diana knows anything about curing transient ischemic attacks?" His words reverberate in the room's vast space. "You know, strokes?"

The concierge shakes his head. "La Contessa has been known less to cure them than to cause them."

Anders swallows hard. "You make her sound like a sorceress—*una strega.*"

"She often has that effect on me," Sebastiano says.

Anders sighs. "Is there a polished shield handy that we can use to see this Medusa, to prevent our hearts from turning to stone?"

"*Mi dispiace*—so sorry, we have no shield," comes a female voice amid staccato footsteps. "I am afraid your hearts will be transformed into stone the instant you gaze upon me—unless, of course, your hearts are already stone."

As if on command, Anders and Sebastiano levitate from their chairs.

Chapter Nine

An elegantly coiffed woman, her silver-streaked blonde hair swept smartly back, enters and walks quickly toward them. She wears a strand of pearls over a black velvet turtleneck, dark gray slacks, and low-heeled, stylish shoes. Anders feels her eyes fasten on him. Even if it weren't for those shining eyes he would know instantly that it was Diana.

"*Un po' vecchio ma meno male,*" she says, stopping to inspect Anders with a curious smile. "A bit old, but not bad, considering," she says, switching to English. "Like a fine Gorgonzola with its green veins showing." She smiles. "Why not speak English, just to show my old teacher how fluent I've become?"

Anders smiles warily. Her impishness has spanned the years intact. He has been wondering how to greet her: whether to bow and kiss her hand with exaggerated respect and irony—or to simply kiss her on both cheeks. Alternatively, he could use his advanced age to bold advantage (and excuse) by taking her in his arms and kissing her lightly on the lips.

The Countess seems to catch a remembered sparkle in his eye. "Ah, Professor Croft, after so many years, I'm afraid much has changed."

Anders stops short and bows his head.

"But please sit down," she says, circling to the couch on the other side of the *pietra dura* table. "Filippo will be here shortly with tea and Campari. There," she says, as they seat themselves, "it is too trying to enjoy afternoon tea standing up." She gives the two men a sharp glance. "So, I am Medusa? Which Medusa?" she asks, raising her eyebrows. "The terrifying one who paralyzes men with fear, or the seductive one who turns them to stone with her beauty?"

Anders clears his throat. "The only sorcery I see here, my Contessa," he murmurs, "is that your beauty is even more bewitching than it was when I last saw you."

"I was bewitching as a teenager?" she says, smiling coolly. "You haven't changed—up to your old tricks." She cocks her head and inspects him. "Sebastiano tells me that you have stopped teaching. I suspect it was less painful to give up teaching the boys than the girls."

Anders, sensing the concierge shifting in his chair, permits himself a mournful smile. "One advantage of old age," he says, "is that there are few still alive who remember the errors of one's youth. As for those few, one hopes for forgiveness."

"Well, I am still alive," she says, lifting her dark brows, "and with an excellent memory. You speak of youth in your forties? That was not youth. You were in *la force de l'âge*, as the French say. I should know, as I am there now." She studies him. "You used to seem quite old to me when you were teaching me English. Imagine if I saw you as you are now," she says, laughing.

Filippo arrives, carrying a tray laden with a cozy-clad teapot, cups and saucers, sugar and milk, glasses, bottles of Campari and soda, and a saucer of orange slices. With accustomed ease he sets the tray in front of the Contessa.

"Ah! Our tea," she says. "I do like the British custom. So warm and civilized, especially when a storm rages outside." She glances at the window as a gust rattles the mullioned panes. "Filippo, *caro,* this is my first English teacher I was telling you about, from years ago. Professor Anders Croft." She turns to Anders. "Please meet my husband, Conte Filippo di San Giorgio."

Anders stares at Filippo. *This* is the Count?

The Count lifts his cap and addresses Anders with a bow and a sly smile. "*Piacere.*" His longish gray hair contrasts with jet-black eyebrows and flashing brown eyes softened with laugh lines.

Anders rises unsteadily and delivers a slight bow, returning Filippo's smile. "*Piacere,*" he murmurs.

"Filippo loves to play masquerade tricks on our guests," Diana says, rolling her eyes. "He should have been named Proteus. He is impossible."

"But...?" Anders begins. "And the gentleman with the dog downstairs?"

"That was Giacomo, our *maggiordomo,*" Filippo replies. "Does he not perfectly resemble a *conte*? He has had years of practice, as I have had years to practice imitating him."

Diana is smiling. "Giacomo is a willing partner in Filippo's jokes. It helps that their clothes fit each other perfectly." She averts her eyes. "My husband's theory is that life is anyway only a matter of playing roles."

"Especially the roles we have so many of inside us, bursting for expression," the Count says, theatrically raising an index finger.

"I understand," Anders says. "Our many *personae.*" Still, he is not sure whether Filippo is being serious or mocking. And just how much has Diana told him about her first English teacher? He turns to Sebastiano. "And here I expected you to warn me about ambushes."

"Then they would be *failed* ambushes," the concierge says slyly. "The prey escapes."

Anders shakes his head. "Imagine Virgil leading Dante straight into Infernal traps."

"But this is not *La Commedia*. And this was only one small ambush, one of temporarily reversed identity."

"I hope it's the only one," Anders murmurs.

"*Caro mio,*" the Contessa says to Filippo, "would you care to change your clothes, then return and join us for tea and Campari? You have been your usual marvelous *maggiordomo*."

With a servant's proper decorum—and a glint in his eyes—Filippo bows. "*Senz'altro, Contessa.*"

"We live in two houses, so to speak," she says as they sit down after Filippo has left. She draws a cigarette out of a small silk purse, pausing to glance at Anders. "You don't mind?"

"Not at all." There was no question, he recalls, of Diana smoking at age sixteen.

"You Americans are so healthy," she says, and lights her cigarette. She draws and exhales a cloud of smoke. "Filippo lives downstairs and I live upstairs. That way our eccentricities don't disturb our domestic *serenità*," she says, her eyes on the bright stones of the small table's surface. She leans forward and taps her cigarette over the ashtray.

"And the role-playing?" Anders asks.

"The playing of roles, as my husband said, fulfills our ever-changing personalities. It also spices a marriage," she says with a small smile.

What, Anders asks himself, could she be speaking of? Switching sex roles, cross-dressing and other perversions? His little Diana? The truth is that he is still trying to recover from the shock of meeting her. At forty-six she is still beautiful and self-possessed. He feels her power and wonders, aware of his beating heart, how much more she is than the plaything she was so long ago. Did he love her more than he realized? Is he again falling under the spell of those quicksilver eyes?

"Don't look so stunned, Professor. I am grown up now, and the world has changed." Her laughter is lightly mocking.

Anders blinks. He does not want to appear defensive or worse, hidebound. He will do his best. "I can only confess that I am impressed by the person you have become, Contessa."

"Oh, life has its effects. And experiences. I went through the sort of *angst* that young people go through, when they do foolish things," she says, giving him a sober glance. "Years pass, things happen. We reflect on past mistakes and learn. I found that with my imagination I could right certain apple carts. I believe that is the correct Anglo-American expression?"

"Yes," Anders answers reflexively, "an excellent use of idiom." Is she reflecting on her past mistakes with *him*? This forty-six-year-old lady must recall every liberty he took with her when she was an impressionable…yes, about her daughter's age now. His face goes hot, and he glances at Sebastiano. "None of this is a surprise to you?"

"That the Contessa is righting certain apple carts?" The concierge lets the question hang in the silence for a moment—purposely, it seems to Anders. "To me it all seems very appropriate."

The Contessa half-closes her eyes as she draws on her cigarette and exhales. "Who would like tea and who would prefer Campari?"

"Campari, *per favore*," the two men say almost in unison.

"Even whiskey," Anders mutters, needing something more bracing, "if you have it."

"No whiskey at the moment, but we could send Giacomo out to fetch some before dinner. Now, who will pour the drinks?"

"Certainly, Contessa," the concierge says, rising. He pours a glass of Campari for Anders and for himself and adds to each a slice of orange.

Diana sips her tea and tips her head back. "And so, cousin, you have had a chance to catch up on things with our old friend?"

Sebastiano lowers his eyes and flushes, as if he is a pupil in the class of an adored but feared teacher. "Yes, cousin."

"Then you have explained that we are expecting him for dinner, and that he will be our guest for the night here in Palazzo San Giorgio?"

"I thought I would allow *you* to do that," the concierge murmurs.

Anders' Campari has gone down the wrong way and he has a coughing spell. Shrugging off their expressions of concern, he finally asks, "I'm to spend the night?"

Diana appears mystified. "Why not? Now, look at you, like a trapped animal—face as red as your drink." Her expression becomes mischievous. "There was a time when you might have leapt at such a chance."

Anders assumes a pained expression. Why is she so obviously baiting him? "I haven't been well, Contessa. It's not just the jet lag. I've been having cerebral ischemic accidents. Little strokes. I will have to get back to the hotel to get some sleep to revive myself."

"Ischemic accidents? My poor Professor," Diana says, her voice softening. "The last thing we want is to endanger your health. We have already arranged for you to take a nap upstairs after we finish our tea. This evening's entertainment has been designed to be therapeutic for you. Perhaps even cathartic."

"Entertainment?" Anders answers, forcing a smile. He sips his drink, avoiding the orange slice. "What sort of entertainment have you designed for an old retired professor who is some-what the worse for wear after a difficult flight?"

She tilts her head and seems to appraise him. "Now that sounds almost self-pitying, as if life has not been kind to you. I originally thought of doing a play—Terence's *Eunuchus*. You could have played the undemanding role of the aging eunuch. Or better, you could have played Gnatho the Flatterer, more suitable but requiring more energy. Do you know the play?"

Anders winces. "I read it long ago, Contessa." Has he detected a hint of malice in Diana? How to deal with it—with diplomacy? "No, Contessa, I cannot deny that I am an old man, but I do not complain. Yet you are still so young. How do you do it?"

"Oh," she laughs, "a contract with the devil."

"I am delighted to see you showing off your English," he says, his heart skipping a beat. "It is so idiomatic, so polished. You should be proud. I remember, when I was teaching you your first idioms, your frustration at all the irregularities in our grammar, so many words with multiple meanings. And now listen to you."

Her face colors slightly. "Ah, my Professor, ever the Gnatho. It is so natural to you that you do it unconsciously, even after I announce your suitability for the role. Be careful. You of all people know where Dante consigned the Flatterers. With the Seducers, if I recall correctly." Her eyes light on Sebastiano. "Did I ever tell you, cousin, how it was that Professor Croft managed to capture my confidence?"

Sebastiano gazes into the depths of his Campari. "Not in detail, cousin."

"No, it would not have been in detail," she says, putting down her teacup and leaning forward with a frown. "Precisely how old was I, Professor? I've lost track."

Anders shifts uncomfortably in his chair.

"I think I will search out Filippo," the concierge says, putting down his drink and rising. "He may need help with his domestic duties."

"My poor cousin," Diana says, after Sebastiano has left the room. "He is too sensitive for his own good. But now that he is gone, Professor, I keep forgetting—how old was I when you taught me English?"

Alone now with Diana, Anders feels more trapped than ever. "It's been so long, Contessa. I, too, have memory lapses."

"Let me see. I believe it was only two years after I graduated from the *scuola elementare*. Does that help?"

"I... I can't..."

"I was sixteen," she says, sighing. "I imagined I was so grown up. Think of it!" She draws on the last of her cigarette, exhales and puts it out. "Ah, you were such a shining light for me," she says. "So paternal."

Paternal? If it is a barb it is lost in a memory that startles Anders by its freshness. It was a late afternoon during the weeks that he, Kate and the children were staying at La Lilia before moving into the Greve house. He had been trying to find Sebastiano to make them a dinner reservation when he thought to check for him behind a door off the lobby marked *PRIVATO*. What he found was a young girl dressed in a white blouse and dark green pleated school skirt sitting alone at a desk doing her homework. She had looked up, startled. "*Scusi—permesso,*" he apologized. Her eyebrows rose..."*Il professore famoso?*" They smiled at each other. Her cousin Sebastiano had told her about him, she said. Disconcerted by the luminosity of her eyes, and their flashing hints of mischief, he had answered in Italian, "No, I'm not famous quite yet." He could think of nothing else to say, he was so transfixed. He could understand why in medieval times it was thought that the eyes saw by beaming rays of light.

"Well, *almost* paternal," Contessa Diana continues. "But who am I to know what a father is? I saw little of mine, busy as he was, operating La Lilia, buying new hotels, and attending to his mistresses." She picks up her teacup and taps its side, as if testing its solidity. "And my loyal mother at home, unaware, or at least pretending to be." She lifts her eyebrows. "How many times did I swear that I would never live my mother's life? That if I could choose, I would choose my father's?"

"I don't recall your talking about that."

"I was vehement about it—all from a little girl's broken heart." She glances at Anders. "But then *il professore famoso* came into my life," she says brightly, "to repair that broken heart. He spoke of teaching me English."

"And I did do that, didn't I?" Anders says, hoping for a fragment of redemption.

"Of course, I continued my English studies after you left, but you gave me a good start," she says, sounding distracted. "But really, wasn't it the secret wish of all of us girls, who were virtually cloistered in those days, that some special man of experience might come along and teach us about his world, the world men owned? And the disappointment when he didn't, when he instead preferred to keep his world secret, buying us off with little gifts, as if our place must be confined to domestic matters? But you, Professor, you took a clever approach. You were only too happy to share your knowledge of the world, preaching of, what did you call them, epiphanies? You began with those of James Joyce, as I recall. Of course your theory of epiphanies was very different from his, and certainly different from the Church's Holy Epiphany, the announcement by the Magi of Christ's Coming. No, your goal was to teach this young Florentine schoolgirl about *secular* epiphanies." Diana nods her head slowly. "*Certo.* You taught me how to achieve *multiple* epiphanies."

Anders feels his face burn and turns his head. "I never claimed to be a priest," he mumbles. "I did my best, considering the situation. And my strong attraction…"

"To me?" She sighs and lights another cigarette. "I suppose I would never claim to have been entirely innocent. Still…" Her voice trails off. "Yes, that is the ultimate excuse, isn't it?" She laughs a high, nervous laugh. "Attraction." She inhales deeply and blows blue smoke into the air overhead.

"An excuse, perhaps," Anders murmurs. "Still, the truth. And the truth can haunt."

The Contessa's quicksilver eyes glitter. "Can it?"

"Can what?" asks the Count. He has appeared at the doorway with Sebastiano, having reclaimed his violet smoking jacket. "Giacomo is angry with me. He claims that I fed Cangrande too many biscuits, and so he is trying to be comforting to the dog, who has a very bad ache in the stomach." He brightens. "I believe I will join you for a drink. Come, Sebastiano." The concierge takes a seat while the Count strides over to the table, pours himself a Campari, and settles on the couch beside his wife. He leans back and grins at the little gathering, as if to claim his share of the secret reason they are all there.

"These Jack Russell terriers have such delicate stomachs," Diana complains to no one in particular. "I warned Filippo. 'Why not a cocker spaniel?' But no, he insisted that terriers are *come si dice*—feistier?"

"*Sono più spiritosi*," Filippo says with authority.

"Filippo, how can a dog be witty?" she says. "People are witty, not dogs."

The Count turns toward her with great dignity. "*Non è vero.* Dogs can be quite witty. Cangrande is *tanto* witty."

The Contessa studies Anders for a moment as she smokes her cigarette. Then she leans back to examine the ceiling's frescoes, a circular sequence of painted mythological scenes. "Professor, do you recall Ovid's *Metamorphoses,* and the story of Myrrha?"

Anders follows her gaze upward. "Myrrha, who fell in love with her father the King?"

"Not only fell in love," she replies, "but consummated her passion for him."

As if on cue, Filippo rises from the couch and gestures toward the ceiling, his chest swelling with pride of ownership. "Our family in the sixteenth century commissioned an artist of the Mannerist School to paint these frescoes, inspired by the *Metamorphoses,* at a time when Ovid was quite *alla moda.*"

"*Sì, caro.* Quite fashionable," Diana says patiently.

Filippo gazes upward as if at heaven. "Venus set the Furies against Myrrha," he adds, "because the girl had refused all suitors, denying the Goddess of Love her due."

"As if refusing suitors isn't the prerogative of any woman," Diana murmurs.

Filippo frowns at her. "Venus would have her revenge," he says as if to a theater audience. "Such a good girl Myrrha was, about to hang herself from shame for her lust for her father. But her nurse from childhood took the rope from her hands." He points upward. "Look at the nurse, whispering in the ear of Myrrha, taking her rope away. 'Why should you die for having such desire?' the nurse says. 'Things can be managed, dear child.'"

Anders peers up at Myrrha's diaphanous blue gown billowing in the winds whipped up by the Furies. "Your Mannerist artist certainly got himself into the spirit of things. I have to admire the delicacy of the painting of the myrrh tree," Anders says, trying to steer the conversation away from the inflammatory subject of sex.

"If I may continue," Filippo intones. "Myrrha's childhood nurse guided her to the King's bed each dark night that his queen was away at celibate worship. Finally the King was so very curious to see the face of the girl the nurse had told him was one of his passionate subjects. He lit a torch and was horrified to see his own daughter. He reached for his sword, but she escaped into the night."

"The tree's fine branches and leaves," Anders continues, gazing upward, "really seem to rustle in the wind, so delicate, so feathery. And it's impressive that the colors have stayed so vibrant over the centuries."

"There," Filippo says, pointing, "is Cupid pleading his innocence to the Gods—that *he* never wounded Myrrha with his arrows. Myrrha is the guilty one, he says, even if his arrows *were* going off in all directions."

"Yes," Diana says, giving Anders a meaningful glance, "Cupid's arrows *did* have a habit of going off in all directions, didn't they? Arrows, one could say, without conscience."

Anders winces. Is the Contessa alluding to their own trysts? He can't shake the memory of his and Diana's fevered couplings in his Alfa Giulia. He must try to put things in perspective. "The ancients," he says, "rarely let conscience get in their way."

"Exactly," she says. "Imagine a noble king, nearly killing his own daughter, furious at being deceived, thinking only of his own honor. A fine father!"

Filippo shakes his head. "*She* was the seducer! But she paid the price. Pregnant, fleeing into exile, she prayed that the gods not let her live *or* die. Instantly dirt covered her shins, roots sprang from her toes, and her bones became like tree trunks."

"*Che orrore!*" Diana says with disgust. "Awful!"

"*Ma che spettacolo!*" Filippo says, his chest swelling with pride. "What a drama!"

"Drama indeed," Anders murmurs. He feels Diana's eyes on him. The air in the room is thick with emotion. Why all this intensity, he wonders, about a mere myth?

Diana turns to Sebastiano. "You haven't said much, cousin."

"I prefer to listen, cousin," he answers, forcing a smile. "I am a listener and a watcher, as at the opera."

"But this is not opera," Filippo mutters.

The concierge's eyes roam the faces circling the table. "For me, all of life is an opera," he says quietly.

Outside, the sound of the storm's whistling surge fills the room. Anders grabs his glass and swallows some Campari. "Why," he says, shaking his head, "would someone commission a fresco on such a delicate subject for a palazzo's *salotto*?"

"Why? Because it is so *lovely*," Filippo says, whispering the last word.

Diana puts out her cigarette, rises, walks to the window, and stares at the storm outside. "But surely you know why, Professor?" she says. "People are fascinated by the forbidden—*especially* by the forbidden. You of all people must know that."

Anders stares at her back, at the contours of her figure. What does Diana see, past those streaks of rain on the glass? Is it a downpour on a mountaintop, two lovers running to a car for shelter, to be quickly in each other's arms? "*Especially* by the forbidden?" he says.

"It is true," Filippo breaks in. "Children most love *il vietato*—the forbidden."

"The Professor only pretends not to know," Diana says, turning away from the window.

Anders assumes a baffled expression, playing for time. The word *forbidden* has triggered a rush of feelings and memories. When he first began spiriting Diana into the hills to make love, he counted on the fact of his marriage and the difference in their ages to spice the affair for her. How attractive the breaking of rules would be to a girl as precocious as Diana, he'd thought—to be lovers united in secret conspiracy.

"What if we're caught?" she had asked one afternoon as she arched herself over him in the Alfa's passenger seat, helping him as he pulled her underwear down. "What about your wife?"

"What about your father?" he'd answered.

"My father *should* find out—it would serve him right," she had replied, her knees clenching his hips,

He remembers the late sun shining through the Alfa's passenger window, filtered by the overhead branches of the acacia, printing a dappled pattern on the curve of her thighs. "Well, if your father caught us," he whispered, as he pulled her down onto him, "you would be in trouble and I might wind up dead." Lost in sensation, she hadn't responded.

Walking away from the rain-swept window, Diana comes toward him now. "I would not mind Myrrha's love so much except for one thing."

"What is that, *cara mia?*" Filippo asks.

"Undoubtedly it was her *father* who lusted for *her*, not the reverse."

"*Per favore?*"

Diana lights a cigarette and blows smoke at the fresco overhead. "The myth-maker was surely a man. Where sin is concerned it is often more convenient for those in charge to blame the victim."

"It's true that certain myths are open to psychological interpretation…" Anders begins.

"I have read," she interrupts, "that the child molester assumes that the child experiences the same lust he does. He tells himself that the *child* seduced *him*. This myth that Ovid collected, so cleverly painted here, has things upside down.

Why, these Ancient Greeks even had Pasiphae wanting to mate with a bull!"

"Well," Anders says quietly, "they believed lustfulness characterized *both* sexes."

"Except that the Greek and Roman mythmakers had their women's lusts run to the bizarre, wouldn't you say?"

Anders bows his head.

Sebastiano seems about to speak, but merely examines his half-empty glass.

A charged silence fills the room, punctuated only by the slapping of raindrops against the windows. Outside, clouds have darkened the sky, deepening the gloom. Nobody moves to turn on a light.

The Count suddenly rises and gives his wife a savage smile. "All of these years you have thought my ancestral fresco a curse on women by men? *'Donne, ch'avete intelletto d'amore.'* You want to think only the worst of men." He spins on his heel and stalks out of the room.

Diana's face flushes. "When he is angry at me he always recites that line from Dante's *La Vita Nuova.* 'Ladies, who have an understanding of love...' Sarcastically, of course."

Anders puts his hand to his forehead. He feels suddenly dizzy. Was it the Campari? "I think it may be time for me to take a nap," he murmurs. "Please forgive me, Contessa."

"Of course," she says, her voice suddenly formal. "You have traveled far to be here, Professore. In distance, and in other ways. I'll call Giacomo to show you upstairs. I'll ask him to give you a glass of water and an aspirin. Unfortunately, the roof above our guest bedrooms is being repaired at the moment, so if you don't mind, you'll be napping in the third floor servants' quarters. It's an old building, you know, and with these rains, certain accommodations must be made."

Chapter Ten

An hour later Anders dreams that he is enrobed on a throne, apparently giving a papal audience. Somewhere in the background an *a cappella* choir chants, '*Amor ch'a nullo amato amar perdona...Love, who excuses no beloved from loving...*' Women of all ages wait in line, one by one, to kiss his ring. A girl with lustrous eyes appears. But she seems disgusted and turns away. He raises his royal miter in warning. She shakes her head. He opens the Great Book of Accounts on the table next to him and lifts a pen. "Heaven or Hell?" he thunders.

Sighing and grimacing, she approaches him. He pulls his robe aside to reveal the papal Ring of the Fisherman impaled on his erect member. She bends and is about to plant a kiss on the ring when a crimson-capped Cardinal appears. It is Sebastiano. He whispers that substituting the Great Book of Accounts for the Bible is the supreme blasphemy. "Promising false redemption in return for fleshly favors," he warns, "will secure His Excellency permanent residence in the Eighth Circle of *L'Inferno*." The Cardinal reaches over and slams the Great Book shut.

At that, a woman's voice rises like a wisp of smoke from the choir. Anders turns at the sound and sees Kate walking toward him. She is bloody and mangled, and her eyes are empty sockets. "*You...you...*" she mumbles through missing teeth and torn lips. She is carrying a knife, the blade of the curved type used for flaying.

"No-o-o-o-o," Anders moans. He struggles awake and heaves himself onto one elbow. He is sweating. Fully clothed, he is lying on a narrow bed in a small, dimly lit, unfamiliar room. The shade over the room's window is drawn. The only furniture besides the bed are a straight-backed chair and a white nightstand. A pitcher of water and a small glass sit on the nightstand, along with a yellow ceramic ashtray. Is he in a cheap hotel? The transition from papal audience is jarring. He is alone—but no, *not* alone. At the foot of his bed someone sits in profile, head bent. A woman. His flesh freezes. Kate? Has he finally died? His eyes strain to see. Though her face is in shadow, he detects a glint—it is her eye, not an empty socket. Her lips are not torn. The woman is watching him out of the corner of her eye. And what is that she is holding—a knife? His heart beats ferociously. No, it is only a bottle, and an envelope. "Who are you?" he croaks.

"If I thought a nap after a Campari would bring you nightmares, I would not have suggested it."

Diana. But is she real? Is he still dreaming? He falls back onto the bed. "*Cara mia,* where am I?" he asks.

"We are upstairs in one of the bedrooms of the servants' quarters. I came up here to give you your whiskey. Remember, you asked for whiskey? Filippo has left us in a sour mood. Whenever we have an argument he runs off to Demetria, his mistress, and complains to her that I am a *stronza*. Do *you* think I am a bitch?"

He rubs his eyes. "What a question," he says. He raises himself, manages to stuff his pillow behind him, and leans back. His mind is re-assembling itself. Shall he tease her? "On the contrary, I have always thought of you as my *Bice*."

118

"Very cunning," she says, shaking her head, "to use Beatrice's nickname. Anyway, with you there were many *Bices*, no? Why do you think I am one of them?"

"You are the only one." He smiles weakly. "I know by your eyes. The way they gleam."

"You can tell I am a *stronza* by my eyes?"

"No, a *Bice! Beatrice!*" He frowns. "You are playing with me."

"As you played with me." She turns away. "I was thinking as we were talking downstairs that you never even knew me. You still don't. When I was sixteen you treated me like a little doll. You wanted only my young body." She glances at the bourbon bottle in her hand. "Filippo is almost right when he says I wish to think only the worst of men, but what he doesn't admit is that the worst is often true. In any case," she says, shrugging, "I am only part bitch. The rest is something else."

Anders tries to gather himself. He is still shaken by his dream's vision of a wraith-like Kate. He feels powerless to prevent this conversation from plunging into areas beyond his control. His first impulse is to deny he never understood her when she was young, but no, he can't recall, just now, what they ever talked about beyond English grammar and vocabulary. Did they share opinions, have arguments, or tell jokes? He knows there must have been something else, but what? What did one say to a teenager? It was all so long ago. "You say I never knew you, but I did, I just can't say how. That was three decades ago. Now you sit here, a strong woman with firm opinions. In those days you were, I don't know, as yet unformed."

"Yes, Professor, I was only an empty vessel, waiting to be filled." She turns toward him. "But men are attracted to empty vessels, aren't they? Especially when the vessels are new and untouched?"

New and untouched? He wants to ask Diana not to call him Professor, but those words, the glimmer in her eyes, they spark an image of Pamphila, seated with her friends in the restaurant. Yes, that is what Diana looked like, all those years ago. The image of her sitting on his bed is intoxicating. "You were very special, that is all I can think to answer. I have memories, you see. The fondest memories."

"No doubt."

"But I have to ask, why did you invite me here? Why do you want to see me? I've stayed at La Lilia a number of times over the past years. Why wait until my life is almost finished?"

"Maybe it is the only time you are alone," she says pointedly. "When Sebastiano told me you were here without a woman, I was...." Diana cocks her ear and listens. From nearby comes a keening sound, rising and falling in pitch. "No, that will be for later."

Anders wonders—was it the sound of the storm, the wind whistling against the windowpanes? A sense of foreboding fills him, like fog rolling in from a dark place. "So you'll make me wait?"

She places the palm of her hand on her forehead and leans over, as if in pain. "Partly, I invited you...I don't know. Let's say, from curiosity."

"About what?"

She glances at him. "About what a man such as yourself has become by a certain age—what he chooses to tell himself about his life's actions with regard to others, his adventures, his exploitations. I'm now about the age you were when you seduced me. I have a perspective I didn't have as a teenager."

Anders stares at her in the darkening room as if across vast space and time. Is this to be an inquisition? What has he done to this woman? What has Sebastiano, to whom he carelessly confided so much over the years, told her about him? She is a stranger, that's what she is. "What are you trying to tell me, Contessa?"

"Ah, now I am the Contessa!" she says, looking away. "Let us simply say that something was unresolved in my mind. If I had waited any longer I might have had to guess matters at your grave," she says, giving him a sidelong glance. "When Sebastiano told me of your arrival yesterday, it seemed an act of providence. Fated, almost."

"You said something was unresolved? What?"

She examines the bottle in her hands, turning it. "You were always a contradiction. You said you adored me, yet you used me. Like my father, who ignored me until he became aware of my marriage prospects. In spite of your insistence, you cannot love women, even though you are drawn to us. Again, like my father." She laughs a dry laugh. "He died some years ago. His heart stopped in scandalous circumstances with some woman. But you are still alive, so I can ask you. Why? Was it always just a primordial impulse to spread your seed? Like a goat?"

Anders feels a flicker of anger. "Why bother to ask?" he says, leaning forward. "You have already judged and condemned me. What is it? Do you need this information as a character study for a play you've decided to write?"

"Please do not pretend personal irrelevance. It is not becoming. Yes, you could be a model for a play, but this time it is life I am interested in, not art."

"At my age and condition nothing is becoming," he says, falling back on his pillow. "If truth be told," he says, staring at the ceiling, "the accident destroyed much of my memory of our love affair, except for scattered visions. I have only a pleasant feeling, a texture, I guess, of our time together. Except for that first time I met you, in the room off the lobby, the surprise in your eyes, our making love in the Alfa...that sort of thing."

"Ah, yes, the Alfa Giulia." She sighs. "Destroyed with the evidence."

"Evidence? Of what?"

"You don't remember, of course. How could you?" she mutters. "Anyway, I had Giacomo go out and fetch you this," she says, holding up the bottle. "Its brand is Old Crow, the only American whiskey on the shelves of our nearest bar. They had evidently had it on the shelf a long time. There's still dust they missed," she says, wiping it. She studies the label. "I thought its name rather appropriate."

The wind moans against the outside sills and sings in the shutter brackets. The sound reminds Anders of the chant of the *a cappella* choir in his dream. "Diana, this morning I woke up hearing '*Amor ch'a nullo amato amar perdona.*'" He squints. "'Love pardons no one loved from returning that love.' Which Canto is that?"

"You, of all people, asking me? '*...mi prese del costui piacer sì forte, che, come vedi, ancor non m'abbandona.*'" She stops. "Now do you remember?"

"'Love has captivated me so strongly that, as you can see, he won't release me.'" He shakes his head. "Or something to that effect. It is Francesca's lament in Hell, giving her profound excuse."

"Yes." Diana laughs softly. "Not long before your accident, on a hot day in July, you and I were on the Prato Magno to escape the heat. You knew I loved the wild lavender. There was a thunderstorm," she says, her voice trailing off. "We had spoken of Dante's adulterers, Paolo and Francesca."

"That I remember," he says, but cautiously, as if the memory might be incriminating. "And the lightning. We were almost killed."

"We were as close as you ever allowed…"

"To death?"

"Death, yes. And to each other. Which might have meant the same to you."

"Blame the accident," he says, not knowing what else to say. It is almost a retort.

She turns and gazes at him steadily, her eyes gleaming in the shadows. "Oh? We might have become closer without the accident? Is that *your* great excuse?"

He averts his eyes under her stare, hating this. How many times in his life has he had to face these recriminations, these accusing fingers pointed at him? "Men and women are different," he mutters.

"Exactly. You never said good-bye."

"But given the nature of our affair, and my physical condition in the hospital, what did you expect? I couldn't even speak, with my jaw wired."

She laughs. "At sixteen I certainly never expected you to invite me into your household as a substitute for a dead Kate, as a mother to your children."

"What then?"

Her shoulders sag. "Never mind." But it seems she hasn't finished. "For years I tried to recapture the passion I had with you that one year. I thought it had to do with you. For years I thought that."

"Yes, that one year. What a grand passion," he says proudly. "But you had doubts?"

"Finally I understood that the passion came not from you. No, it came from inside *me*. The passion was mine." She laughs. "All mine. You were the tool of my fantasies made real. If I hadn't realized that I never could have married Filippo."

He feels confused, even hurt. "I don't understand."

"When I realized the passion was all mine I felt free,

123

dependent on no one. I could do anything I wanted. I could even marry if I so desired."

"Even marry?" He examines her, trying to grasp her words. "The passion all yours? How strange. Then it was no doubt easy to be with other men after me. We were interchangeable, I suppose." He feels an unexpected wave of jealousy, then something like relief, even kinship. "You are more like me than I thought."

"I had to *become* more like you, *Professore*. More like you and the father I had."

"You should call me Anders."

"No," she says after a moment, "I prefer *Professore* and *Contessa*. They sound like the principal characters in a bad play."

Anders realizes he needs a drink. "What if we find a way to open that bottle? I could use a sip. And then perhaps you can tell me about this evidence you say was in the Alfa."

She sighs. "You really don't know, do you?"

"No idea."

"Evidence of our adultery, of course. Mainly yours, since you were the married one, *you* were the Francesca." She shakes her head. "Why am I sitting on your bed, digging up this *roba passata*—our past stuff?" She breaks the seal on the whiskey bottle, unscrews the cap, rises and walks over to the bedside table. She picks up the glass, pours an inch of bourbon, and offers it to him.

"I agree—why are we mulling over this *roba passata*?" he says, maneuvering himself to take the glass. She is close now. The dying afternoon light that creeps in around the shade is softly illuminating her face, creating a Quattrocento Old Master effect. He can smell her perfume, even imagines he can smell her body through the black velvet turtleneck and gray slacks.

He pats the sheet next to his pillow. "Sit down. Yes, we committed adultery. Was that so terrible?"

She reaches for the pitcher. "Water in your whiskey?"

He shakes his head and again pats the sheet.

She puts the glass of bourbon in his hand, sets the bottle next to the pitcher, and reclaims her place at the foot of the bed.

"You should not wish me that close, " she says, her voice trailing off. "Think about that last time we made love in your Alfa Romeo, up in the hills above the city."

"How can I not?" he says after sipping the bourbon, savoring the rich burn. "Why sit so far, Diana? Why all this mystery?"

"Do you recall the fight we had that afternoon?"

He frowns. "There is only one fight I remember and it was not with you."

"It began over a little thing. I wanted to stay there and talk, afterward, be close after having sex. Usually you would zip up and before I knew it we would be driving down the hill again. You would drop me off at the Biblioteca and be on your way to your wife and children." She reaches into her purse for a cigarette. "Normally it didn't matter so much, but that day it did. I had had a fight with my father."

"One of many, I gather?"

"I was feeling vulnerable, a miserable *ragazzina*, a little girl left alone again," she says, lighting up and blowing a cloud of smoke. "I insisted on our staying in the car and talking about things, not just wiping myself clean, physically if not morally, as you started the car. It wasn't my time of the month that made me irritable," she says, gazing at him. "No, it was definitely not. But you were in a hurry, and you lost your temper."

Her words stir in Anders not the memories, but the *feelings* of the memories of that afternoon, locked away. "I must have felt guilt about Kate."

"Well *I* felt discarded. I saw that you didn't care—for you I didn't exist. Usually I swallowed my anger, but this time I didn't. You had gotten what you wanted and wouldn't think of me until the next time you wanted...*scoparmi*—to fuck me."

Anders flinches at the crude *scoparmi*. How strange that such a word comes from the mouth of his little Diana, now a Contessa, he thinks, as her bitter words wash over him. Things are being dislodged in his brain, like stones tumbling down a riverbank into rushing water.

"And so I decided I would get even." She draws on her cigarette and slowly exhales. "Before we made love in the Alfa I would always take off my *mutandine*—my underwear—so that I could climb onto you."

Anders catches his breath at the sound of her voice speaking the words that create that image.

"And then, afterwards I would put them back on."

"Yes?" he says, puzzled.

"This time, in revenge for your losing your temper, I simply pushed them under the seat, next to the box of tissues, where you wouldn't see them. I said to myself, 'I'll let whoever is meant to find them, find them.'"

An icy sensation creeps up his spine. "As far as I know, no one found them."

"Your accident was the next day."

Distractedly, Anders tries to assemble pieces of the puzzle. How do they connect? "You think the accident was caused by your underwear? Your *mutandine* planted some kind of curse on the car?" He shakes his head. "And so you've felt guilty all these years for the curse of your underwear?"

She is silent as her eyes gleam at him through the curling smoke. Then, as if making some key decision, she clasps her hands and stares at them. "Yes, it is silly of me to be so superstitious, to imagine myself responsible for the death of your wife."

"Let me clear your conscience. Kate and I had a fight the night before. We fought almost the whole night. The next day I was exhausted and deranged. I was driving on the *autostrada* and I pulled out to pass." He pauses. There it is again. Somewhere down the hall is the faint sound of someone whimpering—then that strange keening. Is he hallucinating? "What is that?" he asks.

Diana closes her eyes and shakes her head, as if willing the sound, or his question, away. "There were witnesses to your accident," she continues. "They testified about what they saw. There was a police report. The newspapers had a brief account."

Since he remembers none of it, Anders has the sense that Diana is talking about someone *not* him—that this *autostrada* accident happened to a third person. "And what did these newspapers report?"

"That a driver you passed just before the collision said she saw the woman passenger pushing what appeared to be a piece of cloth, maybe a handkerchief, into your face."

"Pushing a handkerchief into my face?" he says slowly, uncomprehending.

"A piece of cloth, blinding you. So that you could not see."

He plumbs his memory, as he has so many times before. Again the chill, creeping up his spine. "I'm sorry. I don't remember."

She shrugs. "My confession is for nothing. Perhaps it is just as well."

"And yet," he says, taking a long sip of his bourbon and swallowing, "I have these dreams. "I had one a little while ago about Kate. She was terribly mangled, as if from the accident." At the memory a tremor shakes him, and the bourbon rocks in his glass. "She seemed vengeful." He is silent as he tries to get a grip on his nerves. He takes another sip and waits for the burn to subside. "Kate seemed to accuse me—her eye sockets staring—as if she could divine the future, the way the ancients believed the blind could. She held a curved blade of the kind you see in paintings, the kind used so often to flay martyrs of the Church."

"So interesting, Anders," she says with a soft smile. "You were always so logical, so authoritative. And now, for one so sophisticated, to see you frightened by a little dream of your wife."

He hears her but his thoughts are far away. "After all these years, I find myself thinking about my death. Seriously. Before, it was not *when* I would die, but almost *if* I would die." He stares at her, wide-eyed. "It is so strange. Just now I dreamed that I was one of the medieval popes Dante chastised for loving worldly things."

"In your case, flesh. The younger the better." Her tone has a mocking edge. "But who will pray for you, Anders? After all, if no one in your family prays for you, you may stay in Purgatory for thousands of years. But no, there is your daughter, Anna. She will pray for you."

"Even if she were my daughter, she would not," he mutters.

"She is not your daughter?" Diana sounds genuinely surprised.

He takes another sip from the glass, swallows, reaches over and places it on the nightstand. His brain is clouding over. Is she pretending not to know after all these years? But how could she have known? "That was what Kate and I fought about the night before the accident. She confessed her infidelity."

Diana says nothing for a minute. "I see. Kate repaid you in her own way."

"Actually, she betrayed me first, when I was in the Army. But it hardly matters now." He appraises Diana's shadowed form doubtfully. "If I am to go to Purgatory, will you pray for me?"

"I might light a candle once a year. That would remove a few weeks from your ten thousand years."

"Ever the tease."

"Not enough in your case." She stares at him. "My question to you is—considering your lofty status as professor, and having had children of your own—why could you never be fatherly to me in the best sense? With understanding and compassion? Why did it always have to be for the purpose of gaining advantage, gaining misplaced trust, so that you might stick your..."

"Please," he says, wincing, as if physically slapped. "Students can be seductive, Diana," he pleads. "As you were with me."

"Even if that were true," she says, her voice rising, "you are supposed to turn it aside. Don't you understand that even more than your charm it was your authority that first seduced me? Yes, of course you do—and did at the time."

He drops his head. "I don't know why I am telling you this but, watching you now, listening to you in the *salotto* a couple of hours ago—I've fallen in love with you all over again."

"Again? There is no again!" She wags her finger at him. "And falling for a forty-six year-old? That is not your style, is it, Professor?"

"For me, you are as you were all those years ago," he says with new intensity. "The same spark, the same *vivacità*, the same *cattiveria*."

"Ah, *now*!" She exhales sharply and laughs. "I am lively and what, naughty? It's only because you are an old *stronzo*. A predator, interested and attracted when the prey puts up a little fight. Yes, I am the prickly sort in this little room, now, where we can call up betrayed confidences. But need I warn you? Outside that door I am Filippo's wife, La Contessa di San Giorgio."

He can't quite tell if she is serious. But he also can't help himself. He has to know. He struggles upright and edges over to where she sits at the end of the bed. She does not move, almost as if she has been expecting this from him. He puts a shaky arm around her, turns her head with his hand, and kisses her. But her lips are not warm and they don't give. They are hard and impervious. He may as well be kissing a marble statue.

She slips out from under his arm and rises to her feet. "Ah, Professor, what made you decide to teach English to a young girl like me? But why ask the fox why he loves the hen? Because she is so intelligent? To improve her? I don't think so. And you always used your left-wing views to camouflage yourself so that you seemed safe, a virtuous academic bestowing justice on humanity, saving the oppressed." She whirls on him. "You say you stand with women—even as you take advantage of us."

Anders is indignant. "I never *camouflaged* myself. I have always been a Marxist and a committed feminist."

She laughs. "You have never been committed to anyone but Anders Croft. If it were fashionable in American universities to be a Nazi, you would have been a Nazi."

He refuses to be ashamed, if only out of pique. "Sebastiano mentioned that you yourself joined the Red Brigades—you became their teenage mascot."

Diana turns and walks slowly to the window, lifts the shade, and gazes out at the rain. "Yes, I flirted with the *Brigate Rosse* when I was seventeen or eighteen. I suppose your left-wing protestations had their effect. I wanted to see what the Left was really like—the Italian Left. I fell for one of them, a good-looking guy with all the answers." She sighs and plays with the shade's cord, the soft light illuminating her strong nose, firm chin, and the glowing pearls that encircle her throat. "They turned out to be revolutionaries who were nothing but misfits.

You had to wipe their noses for them. They were egotists who loved only themselves and their precious ideal of a dictatorship that would impose equality on all, whether the people wanted it or not. And of course *they* would rule this wonderful new system." She turns and studies him. "Your Marxism was different. It was a cunning means to a different end. Yours was the sheepskin the wolf wears."

"That's an unfair conjecture."

"Radicals are all the same. It was easy for the *Brigate Rosse* to shoot Moro and stuff his body into the trunk of that car because they had already disconnected the wires to their own hearts."

"Easy for you to say," he says, feeling himself losing control. "You are an elitist, Contessa di San Giorgio."

"No, Anders, you are the elitist, a self-selected priest of hypocrisy. With your wires, as I said, disconnected. In 1935 Italy you would have worn a Black Shirt, and in the 1965 USSR you would have joined the KGB, if that was where the prettiest women were."

"Not true."

She laughs. "So, I am a liar who is not being fair?" She walks over to the ashtray and stubs out her cigarette, then checks her wristwatch. "What does one do with someone like you?" she mutters. "In any case we will begin the entertainment in less than an hour. Dinner will be at eight." She picks up the envelope and hands it to him. "You may want to familiarize yourself with this. We're going to read from a play I wrote. Don't worry, it's a short one. You'll do well. You have always been a good actor."

Perhaps it is the bourbon, but something gives way in him, like a breath, taken and held too long, finally exhaled. He stares at the envelope, his eyes out of focus. "I don't know if

I am up to it. First, you must tell me why you *really* wanted to see me again."

"Why must I?" She gives him an indefinable look. "You will find out. Perhaps after dinner."

"Diana," he says, turning the envelope over in his hands. "I'm exhausted. I doubt I will be able to go anywhere after dinner."

At the door she glances back at him. "Pamphila will be joining us at dinner. That should revive you. I'll have Sebastiano come for you in a little while. There's a bathroom down the hall, third left, where you can wash," she says before closing the door behind her.

Chapter Eleven

"I'm not up to an amateur play," Anders grumbles as he follows Sebastiano down the narrow stairway from the servants' quarters. His right foot nearly gives way and he clutches the railing. "Slower, Sebastiano, slower. Do you want to kill me?" How ironic, he thinks. Yesterday at dawn, staring out of the bus window on his way to the airport from his Arizona *casita*, he was studying the desert as it stretched off, placid and smooth in all directions. It had seemed to ask, "Why rush? Who cares? It all ends the same." The desert, eroded for millennia by wind and rain, calm in its passive acceptance of geologic time, seemed to mock him. And here he is in Florence, drunk on the brown whiskey he'd contemplated using to end his days after Anna arrived on his doorstep.

Slowed by the Old Crow, he plants each foot carefully, the steps seeming to sink under his feet like small trampolines. With the manila envelope tucked under his left arm, he grabs again at the handrail. At best, Diana's play will be a bore, he has decided. At worst, the bourbon will help.

The concierge glances back at him. He has spruced himself up, his fringes of gray hair slicked down. A yellow silk tie that may be one of Filippo's is knotted at his throat. His eyes are bright behind his glasses. "No, I don't want to kill you, but what do you expect after drinking all that whiskey? I can smell it from here. Is this how you build your courage?"

"I'm only trying to dull my senses to make the next few hours bearable."

"And have you studied your part?" Sebastiano asks. "You will notice she marked it for you."

Again Anders almost slips on a step. "Damn it!" He stops to catch his breath. "My part? What is there to study? I'll just read it. I'm in no shape to memorize anything." In truth, he'd never opened the envelope.

The concierge lingers on a step. "Then why so much whiskey? Are you afraid of a nasty surprise, *una brutta sorpresa?*"

Though the Old Crow has filled Anders with a familiar giddy warmth, it is only a partial anesthesia, only partly concealing his unease. Of *course* he fears a surprise. "Any surprise this evening would be only one of many so far," he growls. "I won't soon forgive you for luring me into all this. And by the way, what are those strange noises down the hall? It sounds like a dying bird, or a caged animal."

"The Contessa often has guests."

"Well this guest must be in a bad way." He stumbles again but catches himself. "How much farther? Where are we headed?"

"To the library, where La Contessa always has her play readings."

"A library? But where?"

"On the *piano nobile,* where we can expect noble entertainment."

"Let's hope so," Anders mutters. Why, he asks himself, as they reach the last steps, is the concierge in such good spirits? Somewhere downstairs he hears music, something early baroque by the sound of the *pizzicato,* the telltale plucked strings. "So, Sebastiano, have you got them playing one of your favorite operas? Something like Monteverdi's *The Return of Ulysses?*"

"More likely *The Return of the Professore*," the concierge replies, glancing back with a sly smile. "But nothing is up to me. La Contessa arranges everything, including the music."

"That's what I'm afraid of."

They make their way down a dark hall and emerge into a large, high-ceilinged room. The music has paused. The windows' floor-length curtains are partly closed. As they approach, Anders glimpses Diana talking to a seated elderly man in an elbow-patched jacket. Filippo sits nearby, staring at the floor. Several well-dressed couples have settled into elegant armchairs in the center of the room, facing forward as if in a theater.

Spotlights mounted high above illuminate three musicians seated at front: a lutist and a cellist, both male, and a female violinist. All are dressed in somber black. They have now begun playing another piece that Anders recognizes as a *gagliarda*, a courtly instrumental dance of the late Renaissance. A slender young woman in a floor-length red satin dress stands to one side, evidently preparing to sing.

Diana breaks off her conversation with the elderly man to greet Anders and Sebastiano. "Professor," Diana says over the music, elegantly tilting her head, "*saluti*—please join us. I see that you did not forget your copy of my play for the reading." Before he can answer, she turns to include the seated elderly man. Anders judges by the man's lined face and the white hair pasted to his skull that he must be in his late eighties. Diana smiles. "Professor, I'm sure you remember Lucas Hawley."

Anders stares, beating back the bourbon haze. "Lucas?" The gaunt old gentleman rising in shaky stages from his chair bears little resemblance to the man he knew by that name.

And yet, as Anders steps forward to shake hands, there is something about the facial expression and the rheumy blue eyes that recall the artist who was the first to introduce him, so long ago, to Italian art. "It's been many years," Anders says, raising his voice, as if Lucas might be hard of hearing, as he grips his old friend's leathery hand.

"Indeed," the man replies. But his eager expression gives way to confusion, as if he is trying to place exactly where and how he knew Anders. "Are you a painter too?" he asks in a wheezy tenor, pumping Anders' hand robotically.

"I gave it a try long ago," Anders replies, "after you let me stay with you in your studio for a few weeks when I was just out of college. We were introduced, you'll remember, by the young woman who later became my wife, Kate Summers. Your families knew each other in Atlanta." He searches Lucas's eyes for a hint of recognition. "Afterwards I went into teaching and lost myself in the academic jungle. I'm still recovering from the experience." There is no shift in Lucas's blank expression. His advanced age seems impervious to the subtleties of self-deprecating humor.

Anders' mind slips back almost fifty years to when Kate asked Lucas if her young friend, Anders Croft, short of funds, could sleep in his studio for a few weeks. Anders can still hear the sound of the metal-framed glass studio door scraping on its concrete sill as Lucas pushed it open at dawn each chilly morning to begin the day at his easel. The chalky scent of the studio and the smell of the oil paint had reminded Anders of his own grandfather's studio when he was little. The old memory is throwing Anders off balance, and he grabs a chair back for support.

Lucas gives him a patronizing smile. "Had a bit too much, eh? Don't drink more than you can hold, my boy. Now we must ready ourselves for the entertainment. I understand they're going to dance." He gives Anders' hand a final squeeze and lowers himself into his chair. Diana gestures Anders toward a chair between Lucas and herself.

"*Cugino*," she says to Sebastiano, "please take the seat behind us." To Anders she whispers, "Pamphila and her Matteo are about to dance for us. Young Matteo is a fine dancer—he studied in Rome. But he is sixteen and shy, so that he only dances for others when Pamphila can persuade him. He agreed to choreograph a tragic *recitativo* by Rovetta of less than fifteen minutes in the tradition of Monteverdi's *Lamento d'Arianna*."

"A little tragedy?" Anders says, shaking his head as he lowers himself into his chair. So Pamphila has a lover. He should have known—the girl is too pretty. The thought ignites a dormant competitive flame. "So, Contessa," he confides, "aren't most male dancers *finocchi*?" The word for gays is out of his mouth before he realizes it.

Diana shoots him a lightning glance. "Pamphila has nothing to be ashamed of. She can also attest that Matteo is anything but a *finocchio*."

He feels his face flush. "*Mi dispiace, Contessa*," he mutters. "Blame the bourbon." He forces a grin. Will his gaffe ruin the civil tone of their upstairs conversation? "Now let's see, where are the performers?"

"They are stretching in the other room," she answers coolly.

Looking around, Anders notices that Filippo is pouting. Is he still upset at Diana's barbs over Myrrha in the *salotto*? The Count has begun staring at the musicians, his dark eyebrows knitted in concentration as if he is using the plangent chords of the *gagliarda* to calm himself. Anders senses a brooding anxiety hanging over the room. What grates on him is that there is a Matteo in Pamphila's life. It is absurd on his part—why shouldn't she have a boyfriend? Yet it is a reflex he can't control.

The musicians finish playing the *gagliarda*. The spotlights illuminate the floor to the right of the musicians. Two figures in black flash forward from behind the audience into the newly lit space. Anders joins in the brief applause. Matteo, playing *Renzo,* gathers Pamphila, playing *Lucia,* to him without quite touching her. Motionless, they gaze into each other's eyes as the string players begin the introduction.

The strings shift from major to minor key. Anders focuses on the apparition of Pamphila—her hair pinned back, ballerina style, her wide, cheek-boned face in profile. Her long slender neck, the delicate lift of her chin, her mother's perfect strong nose, her alabaster skin—it is all of a piece, poised in practiced tension, awaiting release. In Matteo Anders grudgingly sees a youth who could have posed for Donatello's David in the Bargello, his smoothly muscled body exuding careless grace, his face encircled by dark curls, his chin strong, his lips full.

The music stops. For a moment nobody seems to breathe.

The voice of the soprano breaks the spell with her *"Renzo? O sanguinoso, O lagrimato—Oh bloodied, Oh lamented beloved…"*

The lovers melt to the floor, *Renzo* supine, lifeless. *Lucia's* face hovers over his, her eyebrows lifted in grief.

As the violin, cello and plucked lute surge in accompaniment to the swelling and falling of the soprano's lament, *Lucia* and *Renzo* slowly rise, as the strength of her love pours vital breath into his lifeless body. Their limbs mirror each other as they move in dreamlike arabesques across the floor, *Renzo* gradually finding through her his way back to life.

Lucia suddenly stops, motionless. On point she faces the

audience, slowly raising her arms like wings as *Renzo* gently grasps her waist from behind.

Anders' head swims, as it did, once, so many years ago. Again he sees his thirteen-year-old Eleanor in her white dress stepping out from within the doorframe, her arms lifting from her sides. Anders draws a shaking hand across his sweating forehead. What if he had brought himself, at thirteen, to touch his adored Eleanor's hand, to hold her as Matteo is holding Pamphila, to smell her damp hair, to whisper in her ear that he loved her!

Inflamed, he glances around him. Is he giving off a visible aura, a radioactive glow? But nobody has noticed. They seem as mesmerized by the dancers as he is. He feels an intense head-ache coming on, defiling his present emotions with long-buried images: it is his mother, crazed, so many years ago, when he was a teenager. He was driving her at three in the morning to the drying-out facility. The car was filled with the smell of booze and vomit, she was screaming from the back seat, howling at him—*stop this fucking car . . . I carried you in my god-damn belly . . . I gave you life for Christ's sake . . . this is the thanks I get you little bastard . . . dragging me off to get locked up again in a fucking ward to die.*

He had been able keep that car on the road only by fixing in his mind the vision of Eleanor in her white dress, her slender arms rising from her sides like the wings of an angel.

The lovers before him slowly fold back onto the floor. The soprano, in her brilliant red dress, sings, *"Morte, ch'a me ti tolse . . . Death, who has torn me from you . . .* Lucia's lips hover over his open, still ones, her breath *Renzo's* last memory of life's warmth.

When the *recitativo* ends on its note of grief, the silence is interrupted by applause, and stunned murmurs of *"Brava... Bravo!"* Even Filippo is smiling. Anders sits speechless as the young pair rush from the room.

"Pamphila was stunning, wasn't she?" It is Lucas, nudging him. "By the way, Renzo and Lucia are taken from Manzoni's *The Betrothed*."

Anders can only nod.

"Matteo was terrific too," Lucas adds. 'They are meant for each other." He turns in his chair, stiff-necked and slow, to get a good look at Anders. "Our time is over, I'm afraid, and theirs just begun." His face clouds and he frowns. "You do look familiar. What did you say your name was?"

"Anders Croft." Anders forces the words out amid the whiskey-drenched miasma of his headache. "We knew each other at a different time, in another world."

"Perhaps, but in this world I am Angelo," Lucas says, eyes wide.

"Ah, yes? Angelo who?" Anders can barely look at him. The old guy has clearly lost it.

"An old man with a scythe." Lucas winks. "That is *my* role in Diana's play in a few minutes. And yours?"

To be forever at the mercy of others, Anders wants to say. "In Diana's play? No idea," he says, fumbling with his envelope, trying to find the end that opens.

Lucas gives him a pitying stare. "Never mind, too late. If you haven't learned it by now you'll bungle it."

Diana has risen from her chair and made her way to the musicians to have a word with them. To Anders, her elegant Armani outfit lends her an uncanny, sophisticated bearing that is gracious, not at all condescending. The musicians smile and joke with her. She turns, and her eyes fix on him. She seems to read his wandering, disintegrating thoughts. Is it his imagination? Can she detect his wretchedness?

The guests have risen and are chatting. For the reading,

Giacomo, alert *maggiordomo* that he is, has moved the high-backed chairs into a semicircle in the illuminated space where Pamphila and Matteo have just danced.

"I don't recall your being in Diana's last production," Lucas says to Anders in his wheezy voice.

"I've been in Florence less than a day," Anders mutters, dragging himself out of his slough. "What production are you speaking of?"

"She called it *L'Amore Strozzato*."

Strangled love? Yes, he knows a thing or two about that. "What was it like?"

"It's a sort of historical tragedy...mainly to do with Thais, the Athenian courtesan of Alexander the Great. They say she dared him to burn down the old Persian capital...I can't quite remember the name."

"Persepolis," Anders says.

"Anyway, he took the dare, and she threw the first torch. Dante assigned her to hell for the sin of flattery, for her...her fawning behavior with Alexander." He smiles. "Diana defended Thais, implying Alexander manipulated *her* through her love for him."

The old guy is getting on Anders' nerves. "It does sound like a subject Diana would pick."

"Well, take it from me, Diana made the play work." Lucas looks at him askance, as if sizing him up. "I've known Diana for years, you know. Decades."

Anders takes a deep breath. "So have I. In fact I'm the one who introduced you to her, just as Kate Summers introduced me to you."

The older man gives him a curled-lip look of disbelief. "You said you've only been here a day."

Anders gives up trying to explain—the old fellow's lost his

marbles. He struggles again with the manila envelope. He is beginning to worry what it might contain. Will he have to impersonate a charlatan, or a nincompoop? "Do you know," he asks Lucas, "what *this* play's about?"

Lucas widens his eyes as if in surprised recognition. "This one? She wrote it years ago and updated it for today. So she said. I'm to be Angelo."

"Yes, you mentioned that," Anders says, finally getting the envelope open. He peers at the print, barely able to make out the title: "*The Plague*," he mumbles to himself. "And it's in English."

"She wrote it early on, when she was perfecting her English at school, not long after her lessons with a . . . an unprincipled American, who claimed to be an English teacher."

Anders gives Lucas a quick glance, but the old man seems incapable of innuendo.

By this time their hostess is standing before them all, smiling expectantly. "*Amici miei*," Diana begins, "thank you for coming this evening to read my modest amateur production. You will have noticed it is in English, written years ago when I was studying the language. I brought it up to date in the last few days when I learned that our special guest, Professor Anders Croft, would be visiting Florence and perhaps might join us. It is not in English by accident; it is to honor him as my first English teacher," she says, giving Anders a brief smile. "I made sure to invite you all, my English-speaking Florentine friends. Please welcome Professor Croft."

Anders nods graciously left and right, past Lucas's glare, grateful that Diana's smile is appropriate for a simple introduction. His headache is pounding and his upper lip is twitching.

"Now," Diana says, "if the readers will come forward and seat themselves under the lights. I have cast our good friend

Lucas Hawley as Angelo della Morte. Our visiting professor, Dr. Croft, is Sindaco Don Rodrigo, mayor of the stricken town of Monte Chiana. Pamphila, you will be Angela. Filippo, dear, you will read the stage directions."

Anders follows the others to the chairs. He comes to life as he realizes that the last chair is between Pamphila—still wearing the form-fitting black outfit she danced in—and her mother. Pretending to be unfazed, he sits down and fusses with his script. He finds the throb of his headache already receding. Is it the healing effect of a magnetic field between two deities?

Chapter Twelve

"We find ourselves," Diana explains, "in a four-teenth century town stricken by one of the terrible plagues that regularly swept Italy in those days. The inhabitants are dead or dying. The only person untouched is the mayor, Sindaco Don Rodrigo. He has taken refuge from the catastrophe in the hills above the town in the *castello* he appropriated years earlier when the eighth *Marchese di San Clemente* died under mysterious circumstances. Don Rodrigo hears someone below knocking on his castle's massive oak door."

Rodrigo: (eating dinner alone by torch-
    light in the refectory) Che cosa! Who
    could that be? Some dying fool beg-
    ging for a place to stay for the night?
    (He calls out) Tonino! Tonino! I for-
    got. He's dead too. I must do everything
    these days. Now who would dare disturb
    me at dinner? (Draws his sword, descends
    the broad stone staircase to the main
    hall, removes the iron bar, and drags
    open the heavy door. He sees a dark fig-
    ure standing by the gate) Who is there?

Angelo: (his voice muffled) Angelo.

Rodrigo: Angelo? Angelo who? How have you escaped the plague?

Angelo: Wherever the plague goes, I follow. I do not avoid it.

Rodrigo: Ha! What are you, a gravedigger?

Angelo: But for me the gravedigger would be idle.

Rodrigo: (gripping his sword tightly) You sound like a brigand. Come one step closer, brigand, and you'll find my sword a spit on which I'll roast you.

Angelo: I am no brigand, Don Rodrigo. I am Angelo della Morte. I have come for you, since no one else in this region breathes any longer. You are the last.

Rodrigo: (stepping backward) You call yourself the Angel of Death? Prove it. Prove that you are no imposter!

Angelo: If you wish. (flings his black cape into the air causing an inferno of fire to blast heavenward)

Rodrigo: (chastened) Why—why are you here, Angelo? I have done you no wrong. You have no cause to come for me.

Angelo: There is never cause. There is only time. Did you think you would live forever?

Rodrigo: Angelo, let us discuss this like civilized people. You and I are men of stature. Not plebeians.

Angelo: Men of stature, you say? First, what makes you think I am a man?

Rodrigo: Your name is Angelo, not Angela.

Angelo: Only if I choose. In fact now…(he turns his back to Rodrigo and reappears—Pamphila takes over from Lucas)…I am Angela della Morte. I laugh at you, Don Rodrigo. A lady Angel of Death laughs at you.

Rodrigo: (furious) You are the spawn of Satan. I attack you (plunges his sword into Angela, but his blade finds only smoke).

Angela: Now do you understand? You might ask why I have saved you for last.

Rodrigo: (terrified) Why? What have I done? I have served the town of Monte Chiana faithfully as its mayor. The townspeople look up to me as their noble leader and defender. Or they did when they were alive. I am a good man. Signorina, I am a man of the people.

Angela: You refer to me as a mere "Signorina?" To one who is millions of years old? You call yourself a man of the people but you are only a fraud. You told them you wanted equality for all. You said you were holier than the priest, that you would be the peoples' savior, even as you seduced the men's wives—even their young virgin daughters. As soon as Marchese di San Clemente was in his grave you moved into his castello, demanding legge signore,

146

the sexual prerogative with new brides.
Half the children dying in the hovels
out there are your children. You are no
better than the Marchese. Yes, Sindaco
Don Rodrigo, Mayor of Monte Chiana, you
have served your citizens well.

Rodrigo: (smiling) Yet now you are a woman.
I like dealing with women. In fact, I
prefer it. Women have an understanding of
love, as our great poet wrote. (he takes
a step toward Angela) I suspect that
under that cloak is the lovely figure of a
woman capable of the love and affection of
which I also am capable.

Angela: Yes, I am so beautiful. Look at
me! (she throws back her hood).

Rodrigo: (staggers back, crosses himself)
I...I cannot.

Angela: Kiss me, you Lothario, you Casanova. You will find no red lips covering
these granite teeth of mine. They are
as cold as your favorite gelato, though
not as sweet. Come, kiss these grinning
fangs.

Rodrigo: (trying to recover) But you say
you have come for me! Darling, I love all
women. A million wrinkled years is nothing to me. Even beauty means nothing to
me. It is the female soul I love.

Angela: Ha! So, that is what you crave?
Come, kiss my soul. I will breathe it
past your parted lips into your beating

lover's heart. (she takes a step toward
him) What are you waiting for? Are you
jealous, that I have kissed so many
already? So many of your fellow citizens—men, women, children—have tasted my
breath? Do not be jealous, my darling.
Such a human emotion lasts only moments.
Rodrigo: (turning and running back through
the castle doorway) Away! Get away!
(slams shut the great door, replaces the
iron bar, only to find Angela next to
him).
Angela: You try to escape my embrace, Don
Rodrigo, but my passion is too great.
(throws off her cloak, takes him in her
bony arms and kisses him—he drops, dead
as stone). (To the audience) See how he
swoons, overwhelmed by the attentions of
so great a lover as I. (bows)

Applause breaks the silence. Anders coughs and clears his
throat. His headache is worse again. He hasn't had so much to
drink that he hasn't caught Diana's message. He has to admit
that her English is impressive. But he is upset that darling Pamphila had to play such a monster—the dissonance of it all. He
will pretend that he noticed nothing of himself in the skit. He
leans toward Diana.

"*Brava, Contessa*—your English is masterful! As for your
plot, so much for corrupt, fourteenth century aristocracy."

Diana glances at him out of the corner of her eye. "*Grazie,* my
dear *Professore,* for your honest opinion. I'm afraid there are
many Don Rodrigos in positions of authority to this very day."

"No, not possible," Anders says, laughing.

"Even among *us, Professore*."

"If so, they are well camouflaged," Anders says, hoping to put an end to the subject.

"So they are."

Lucas, who has been listening to them, shakes his head. "Diana, *cara mia*, how did you manage to create such characters? They seem so real. Have you been researching the Middle Ages?"

"No need, Lucas. Some things never change."

Anders flinches. Diana's insinuations are grating. For peace of mind he must ignore them. But his obstinate memory flies back to a certain, long-ago day of his Medieval Theology seminar. Niven has just died. He almost canceled the class, devastated as he is. The news of her death has raced through the university. As he sets down his books he glances up at his students seated around the long table. He reads the condemnation on their faces. "I grieve," he begins, "as I'm sure you all do, at the dreadful accident that has taken Niven from us." The room is so silent that Anders can hear Simon Welch through the wall next door quoting the Pardoner in his Chaucer seminar. Cheryl Robbins, one of his brightest students, rises from her seat. A cheerful, chubby, blonde, her face is puffy and red from crying. She was Niven's close friend. "If I had a gun now, and the nerve, I would shoot you, Dr. Croft," she blurts. "Taking advantage of a girl less than half your age, the least you could do is not *kill* her."

Anders pulls himself back to the present, and scans the faces of the Florentines surrounding him. What do these people know of his life's trials? Certainly at his age he lacks the ability he once took for granted to offer the world an existential shrug and move on. He feels like an old boar finally cornered, *un cinghiale intrappolato*, as the Italians would say, brought to

bay by hungry hounds. He glances at Pamphila. Is it his imagination, or is her face especially pale? Has Diana filled her in
on the history he and her mother share? Did Pamphila play the
role of Angela with that history in mind?

Anders sinks back in his chair. The warm compliments to
Diana for her play are still flowing. The smiling, the murmurs
of *"Brava, Contessa, brava"* continue. One of the invited guests,
a short balding man with a well-trimmed black goatee, has
tipped his head back to study the American professor. "Diana
has demonstrated her usual good form, " he says. "But you too,
Professor—*Bella forma, anche brutto.*"

Anders nods with a forced smile. Good form, the man says?
Also ugly? Do they understand what Diana has done, using
Don Rodrigo to throw dirt on his own difficult past? How
much do they know about him? No, the man must mean that
he did a good job acting the part of an ugly *character.*

Another man about his own age, with a widow's peak,
soaring temples, and a parchment-colored face, is giving him
a knowing smile. "You know, of course, the Don Rodrigo of
Manzoni's *I Promessi Sposi,* Professor? The most famous and
despicable villain in Italian literature?"

Anders smiles gamely. "Yes, of course. Manzoni's *The
Betrothed.* The novel's sinister Baron Don Rodrigo, lusting
after the young Lucia, who loves only her cherished Renzo."

"A fitting end for the Don Rodrigo we all know," a well-
dressed woman mutters.

"*Si,* evil unaware of its own evil."

"What were you trying to tell us in this work of yours,
Diana?" asks another.

Diana hesitates. "Simply to show that Don Rodrigos exist
across all lands and ages—even now. There are plenty of them,
not just in the fourteenth century."

Anders leans toward her. "Is this why you invited me," he whispers, "to the Palazzo San Giorgio, to use me as an example in your morality play?"

"So you think this play was about you?" she whispers with a glint in her eye. "You must think you deserve it. But let me introduce you to the gentleman who mentioned Manzoni's novel. He respects Don Rodrigo as much as he admires the ideas in Machiavelli's *The Prince*."

"Professor Croft," she says, turning, "please meet *il Dottor* Giovanni Corsini, the President of our *Società Drammatica Fiorentina*."

Corsini, the parchment-faced man with the soaring temples and the crafty smile, accepts Anders' offered handshake. "*Piacere*—my pleasure," he says, in his deep baritone.

Corsini turns to address the others. "*Signore e signori, la nostra Contessa di San Giorgio* has again given us a special entertainment. Professor Croft, we are indebted to your participation. Success of such a work, as always, depends on the talent with which the principal actor pretends he doesn't realize that moments of his past history are central to the play's moral message. Having read the play in advance, you knew this, and you turned it to your ironic advantage." He gives Anders a warm smile. "*Grazie*, Professor, for your contribution to La Contessa's artistry."

Anders searches through the ashes of the last few minutes for an explanation of Corsini's strange courtesy. Is this the man's way of smoothing things over so that the victim will cause no further unpleasantness? As for Diana, does she know her old lover so well that she could count on his not reading the play beforehand? And their praise—is it a subtle trick, pretending praise to sharpen his humiliation?

He smiles crookedly at Corsini. It is the kind of game Italians are good at—the creation of complex possibilities, subtly inter-locking contingencies, and the intellectual sleight-of-hand that leaves the possibility of revealing true intent an accident. Is he being praised or mocked? It is not clear and may never be, and so he will suspend a show of appreciation, as well as any sign he feels ensnared.

"After all," Corsini continues, "we all have our faults, do we not? Hasn't each of us, at one time or another, crossed bound-aries of civility, if not humanity?" He smiles broadly, his palms open in a gesture that hints at a gracious accommodation to life's realities. "This is what makes our theatrical attempts so fascinating—the dramatization of the complexity of human nature, and its susceptibility to evil. Professor Croft, I believe we understand each other."

What is it, Anders asks himself, as he listens to Corsini's icy portrayal of the *Società's modus operandi*, about the man's soaring temples and widow's peak? All he needs are horns and a cape. But why is Diana a member of such a society? Is *she* the one who has gotten her wires disconnected along the way? He needs more bourbon, but his Old Crow is upstairs. Can he make it upstairs to his bottle? But Diana is making a sign to Giacomo. Too late, dinner is announced. "Whatever else is on the table," he mutters to himself, "at least there should be plenty of wine."

Half an hour later, Anders' spirits have been revived by mor-sels of *porchetta*—roast suckling pig stuffed with rosemary and garlic—washed down with excellent red wine from the San Giorgio vineyard in the Valdarno. The aroma of the meat alone has worked magic on his memory. It was years ago on market day in Greve that the vendor, with his lightly crusted *porchetta* on its steel spit, was the center of hungry attention.

Toothless old men stood by, grinning vicariously at those who could still chew.

Anders checks his dinner partners out of the corner of his eye. Will things be more pleasant now that they've had their fun with him? Diana, at the head of the table, has seated him to her right, the place of honor, with Corsini on her left. Corsini's wife, Laura, a bright-eyed buxom blonde sitting to Anders' right, is throwing sidelong glances at Matteo, who slouches next to her. The youth is clearly bored, and he throws reproachful glances at Pamphila, opposite him, trying to catch her eye. But Pamphila is in conversation with Santanelli, an old lawyer who stares at her greedily as he pulls at his black goatee.

On Matteo's other side is Santanelli's wife, Mara, a waifish lady with wire-rim glasses, who is having no more luck than Laura Corsini with the young dancer, who is giving her only monosyllable responses. Opposite Mara is Antonella Baldi, a heavy-set woman with a round face and short gray hair. Her husband Claudio, on Mara's right, is an ascetic-looking banker with a greenish pallor, hunched over his food like a praying mantis. At that end of the table, a confused-looking Lucas seems to be sputtering at an impassive Sebastiano while Filippo, next to him, looks away disinterestedly.

"What crimes," Corsini is asking in his cultivated baritone, "did our friend Don Rodrigo really commit in Diana's *schema*? Yes, he spread his seed in the manner of a typical *signore*, but he otherwise followed the logical rules of Machiavelli. A prince cannot be softhearted. He must rule with an iron hand, or he will soon be replaced."

"What are you saying, Giovanni?" Diana says as she signals to Giacomo to refill the wine glasses. "Are you saying it is fine for a *signore* to pretend to be a good man, to preach brotherly love and equality, only to brutalize his subjects, to lure the men's wives and innocent daughters into his bed through fear of his authority?"

"Why Diana, I would never say such a thing—certainly not in those terms," Corsini replies. "For one thing, love and seduction are mysteries. Who can say why a lady, or a girl for that matter, should feel impelled to obey her own desires? True, authority can be an aphrodisiac to women—even married women. But should a ruler stifle his strong male instincts in the interest of civility? No, such restraint would impinge on the popular image of his virility. *Il Duce*, for example, understood this."

"Your admiration of Mussolini is regrettable, Giovanni," Diana says, shaking her head. "But what of the hypocritical ruler who at first pretends to believe that all are of equal value, men and women, rich and poor, and that he is no better than they. Then, when he gets his hands on power, he reveals that it was all an act, that his real heroes are Nero and Caligula?"

"My dear Diana," Corsini sniffs, "a man must do whatever he can to become and remain a prince. If he pulls it off, it is proof of his superiority."

"*Ma Giovanni*," a voice erupts to Anders' right. It is Laura Corsini, her black eyes flashing. "You always talk as if you are a great leader yourself. An *Il Duce* of the operating room." She is wagging her finger at him. "There are plenty of little Benitos nowadays, and where do you think they are? They are in jail!"

Everybody in earshot laughs.

"My wife has a sense of humor," Corsini murmurs to Anders, "and I indulge her." He drains what wine remains in his glass. "But back to Don Rodrigo. Let us say that our sweet Pamphila here," gesturing toward her with a courtly sweep of his hand, "was the object of his affections all those years ago. My dear, how would you parry his predatory advances?"

Pamphila has seemed to follow the argument back and forth, and now her young face flushes beneath the sudden attention. "I suppose it wouldn't matter," she begins in a low voice, "if we take the playwright Pirandello's point of view."

"Pirandello?" someone says in surprise. "Really? It wouldn't matter?" It is Santanelli. He seems amused, or at least prepared to be so. "So you have been taking classes in literature?"

Anders has been furtively glancing at Pamphila across the table, watching her pick at her food, sip her wine, until now silent and listening. Yes, she is the living image of her own mother when she was a fresh sixteen-year-old beside him in the hills above Florence thirty years ago.

"As a character of fiction, Don Rodrigo is eternal and unchanging," Pamphila says, frowning in concentration. "He lives forever as Manzoni describes him. But you and I are short-lived. We turn to dust more quickly than the book describing Don Rodrigo's wickedness."

"And so?" Laura Corsini says, smiling. "How would you react to Don Rodrigo's advances?"

"Not being a fictional character myself, I could accept or reject him" she sniffs, "depending on whether he was good-looking and I fell for him or whether he was hairy and smelled bad." She smiles down at her plate. "But as I said, it wouldn't matter either way, because as a Pirandello character says, we living are the stuff of nothing. Just as I am not now what I was, and am not what I will be in a year, or in a minute. I live and change and die, while Don Rodrigo, the character, is immortal."

There is a small silence. The whole table has been listening.

"*Eccellente!*" It is Filippo, beaming, from the other end of the table. "I am so happy that you have been paying attention to your lessons after all. *Complimenti!*"

Out of the corner of his eye Anders notices Matteo smile.

"But," the young man asks Pamphila, mischievously, "aren't you avoiding the question? What if Don Rodrigo *was* alive, able to change and die—and deceive—and he was sitting here at this table eating and drinking wine? And he made a certain proposition?"

Anders finds Pamphila staring directly at him, a gaze so penetrating, so intense, that he feels himself shrinking. Why is she staring at *him*, as if he is a modern Don Rodrigo? No, his face must be only a moment's resting point for her quicksilver eyes, her mind elsewhere.

Pamphila colors slightly and turns to Matteo. "You and I just danced the Rovetta *recitativo*. Perhaps Lucia accepted Renzo's advances only because he was a good dancer." She is laughing now. "If Don Rodrigo danced better than Renzo, who knows? I might just encourage him," she says, giving her boyfriend a careless toss of her head.

Everybody laughs and there are cries of *"tanto spiritosa."*

Anders feels a chill in his gut at the exchange between the girl and the boy. There was a time when he flirted like this, a time when he could hold a pretty woman's glance.

"*Professore, volevo dire...*" a feminine voice next to him says. "It happens that I *prefer* the Don Rodrigos of this world." It is the blonde Laura Corsini at his right elbow, sliding him a coquettish glance. "Men who are bold, not afraid to make trouble—such men please me."

"Really?" Anders says, awed that a ray of sunshine has penetrated his gloom.

"In fact, I would not be surprised if you yourself seduced and abandoned a lady or two," she says under her breath.

"If so," he says, rising to the occasion, "I would not be so inconsiderate as to abandon her. I would lock her in the keep of my *castello* and subject her to all the torments of love."

Laura Corsini smiles and averts her eyes. "And how long will you be visiting Florence, *Professore?*"

"Indefinitely, my dear Signora," he says, glancing at Corsini, who appears deep in conversation with Diana. "Perhaps one day you and I might go for a drive, an afternoon inhaling the scent of the wild lavender on the Prato Magno—and enjoy a bottle of fine wine?"

"*La prossima settimana*—next week Giovanni will be at a conference," she murmurs, her eyes on her plate.

"*La prossima settimana?*" Corsini is smiling broadly at his wife. "Next week?" He apparently heard his name spoken, and his smile implies he knows his wife well. "And so what is going to happen next week?"

"*Ma niente, Giovanni*," she says, her full lower lip pushed into a pout. "Nothing."

"I am so glad it is nothing," says her husband.

There is a silent pause as those who caught the interplay are staring at Anders and the Corsinis.

Anders' spirits sink. Events seem to conspire against him. He has lost once again.

Diana seems to grasp the situation, because she is smiling. She waits a while for everyone to finish their food and wine, before she makes a sign to Giacomo to clear the dishes, to bring the cheese and fruit. "*Formaggio e frutta, per favore.*"

Anders frowns. Did he just hear Diana call for the cheese and the fruit? Giacomo hasn't heard her, but Anders remembers Dante's mention of Frate Alberigo's signal for the slaughter of his guests, so many centuries ago, in the *Inferno*. It is absurd to imagine the winsome Diana an evil Alberigo, but in his peculiar state of mind, with these cynical guests, it is an omen. Yes, she *has* called for the cheese and fruit, hasn't she?

Anders scans the faces around him. Everyone is laughing—at

him? Why are Santanelli and Baldi-the-Praying-Mantis secretly whispering to each other as they glance at the *professore americano*? That they have made a fool of him—or that he has made a fool of himself? Is he imagining it? Yes, down at the other end they, too, are laughing and whispering. He takes a corner of his napkin and wipes the sweat from his forehead. His hand is shaking badly. They undoubtedly see that shaking, and mock him for it. They are sure he is afraid they will murder him in a dark corner of the Palazzo San Giorgio.

"Anders, are you all right?"

It is Diana, staring at him with concern. *Feigned* concern? He holds her eyes with his to detect a sign—a glint of irony or sarcasm—that would give her game away. But she is too convincing, and so he must also be convincing.

"No, Contessa, all is fine," he says, forcing a grin. "What a lovely dinner. I say that not in surprise, of course, but in appreciation."

Diana's eyes linger on him for another moment before she searches out Giacomo, who is standing by the long walnut sideboard. She motions to him and he comes close. *"Ancora, le frutta e formaggio, per favore,"* she whispers to him.

"Sì, Contessa."

"With Giacomo one must sometimes ask twice," she says, glancing at Anders. "You know, you really do not look well."

He forces himself to laugh. "When you asked for the fruit course, and the cheese. I remembered '*quel da le frutta del mal orto.*' Silly, no?"

Diana throws him a shocked look. "You speak of Frate Alberigo and the fruits of his evil garden? The cutting of his brother's and nephew's throats? You *must* be ill. Look how you are perspiring. Your face is soaking wet. Even your throat..."

"My throat?"

"Anders! No assassins are coming for you!" She gives him a hard stare. "If you want me to show you why I invited you to my home, you must pull yourself together."

Her tone brings him back to himself. "I have this fear—why you invited me," he whispers. "For vengeance."

"Anders! A *vendetta* is beyond me. I admit my play was provocative, but its purpose was to make you understand. To prepare you for what follows."

"You mean this dinner party?"

"For what *follows* this dinner party."

Something urgently personal in Diana's tone catches his attention, as if she is going to ask something important of him. He turns to his now refilled wine glass.

After the wine, after the red grapes and ripe pears that accompanied the Gorgonzola, after the glasses of fine grappa, and after the cups of espresso, the guests begin to depart. Diana escorts them to the door, murmuring *arrivederci*. Only then does she take Anders by the hand. "There is someone I want you to meet."

"Someone else?" he asks.

"Yes, someone else."

Chapter Thirteen

It is a long climb up the stairs to the third floor. Anders' right foot slips several times. He is sluggish from the throat-burning grappa. The espresso helped clear his head, but he is experiencing a strange sense of being divorced from his surroundings, as if he should not be here in this place. He strains to lift his legs from step to step.

Is his discomfort due to having drunk too much? Surely not all of it. And where is Diana leading him, in his distressed, ine-briated state? Back to his napping place, his bedroom? Who knows what might happen with his lovely ex-lover? But he must stop for breath. His once capacious lungs and strong heart are not what they used to be.

"Only a little farther." It is Diana's voice, directing him, *pull-ing* him upward.

Her voice sounds so solemn, he thinks, as they reach the next floor. Anders leans against the wall for a moment. "My room is nearby," he says. "Care for a nip of Old Crow, *cara mia?*"

Diana ventures very close, inches from his face, and stares into his eyes. "That is not why we are here, Anders."

"Oh?" There is a reason they have climbed up here, but he has misplaced it. Being alone with the magnetic Diana must account for his fuzzy-mindedness. Even her secretiveness is enchanting.

"Come," she says, taking him by the hand and leading him down the hallway to a closed door. She stops and turns to him. "We are not acting parts in a play, Anders. Unlike Pirandello's characters, we're alive and in the present." She seems small and alone as she stands there, studying him. "Are you ready?"

Only now is he filled with apprehension. Not because of her words, but by the stoniness of her expression in the semidarkness.

Diana opens the door to a small, narrow room much like the one in which he took his nap. There is the faint smell of urine. On a bedside table a lit lamp only accentuates the gloom. Someone is in the bed, a face on a pillow. Opposite the bed an old woman, white-haired and small, sits on a chair. She turns her head as Diana and Anders enter.

"*Grazie, Bianca. Ci puoi lasciare per pochi minuti,*" she says, asking her to leave for a few minutes.

"*Grazie a lei, Signora,*" the woman says, rising stiffly from her chair and leaving, softly closes the door behind her.

The face on the pillow turns and makes a strange keening sound, like the cry of a bird.

"Anders, I want you to meet Teresa," Diana says. "She is a person who entered this life under the worst of circumstances. How much she suffers is impossible to know since she cannot communicate with us, though she is an adult. Her mother gave birth to her out of wedlock on a farm in the small town of Gavorrano in Maremma. Whether it was the midwife's fault, nobody knows. The birth process was difficult. The baby became, *come si dice,* lodged in the birth canal, the placenta was torn, and the supply of oxygen to the baby's brain was cut for at least eight minutes, maybe more. In the many years since, she has never spoken any word or given any indication that she understands any. She cannot walk, sit upright, or do anything but lie in bed. Bianca turns her twice a day to prevent bedsores. We feed her intravenously."

Anders is aghast. Now that his eyes have adjusted to the dim light, he makes out the incessantly rolling eyes below the neatly combed hair in the blotched red face on the pillow. Something in his soul stops still.

"Over time her arm and leg bones, because there is no muscle tone, gradually rotate and dislocate out of their sockets. Every five or six years the surgeons must operate to relocate them. This causes her great pain, and for weeks she screams, not understanding what has happened to her."

"This is horrible, Diana," Anders mumbles, barely able to speak. "Where is her mother? Why do you have to take care of her?"

Diana sits on the side of the bed and begins to stroke the blotched red forehead, which evokes an instant response, a kind of whimpering, a working of the lips, a tossing of the head from side to side. "The mother was very young when she became pregnant, and was forced to visit friends of relatives in Maremma to have the child so that her family would not be scandalized. This happened in a time when pregnancy out of wedlock was shameful, disallowed. Today people look the other way, or even celebrate."

"But why you? Why must *you* care for Teresa?"

Diana turns to look at him. "Because Teresa is my daughter. *And yours.*"

Anders frowns at her. "What did you say?"

"Your daughter, Anders. That last time we were together. Up on the mountain. The wild lavender. The storm. Your Alfa. You remember, don't you?"

He stares at her. "This woman in this bed—she was conceived that day? She is our child?"

"Yes, Anders."

He turns, makes his way across the room, and carefully lowers himself into the nurse's chair. "Why," he whispers, "didn't you let me know?"

"For what purpose? What would you have done? Besides, this is Italy, Anders. I was just seventeen. My father was beside himself. He would have killed you. I could do nothing."

"But I might have…"

"You might have what? Everything is done. Teresa is thirty years old. She was in a hospital for the first twelve, then with the nuns. I couldn't bear it. I finally convinced Filippo to let her come to live with us. I pay for her nursing, of course. He agreed, as long as friends think she is the daughter of a distant Maremmano relative. Though I have told him otherwise, Lucas still believes she is his, since we were together a few weeks after you left." She reaches out her hand. "Come, Anders, greet your daughter. Say something to her. She feels your presence. She hears your voice."

Anders gets up, goes over to the bed, and stares at the face on the pillow. "My daughter?"

"I never stop wondering what life for Teresa is like," Diana says softly. "What does she think? Does she dream? What could her dreams be? They couldn't be the dreams you and I have, of walking by cool streams in the Casentino. Or even nightmares, at least as we know them. She knows neither the best nor the worst of this world."

The expression on Teresa's face seems to Anders one of intense interest. Her breathing has paused, and her eyes are wide. It is clear she *has* heard a different voice, one she has never heard before.

Anders tries to get his bearings. He watches Diana stroke Teresa's forehead over and over. It seems incomprehensible.

"My God, what have I done?" he says, his voice shaking. "This is my child? This poor woman is my daughter? What can I do?" He takes a step back, for what reason he doesn't know. The room slips sideways, turns upside down, goes black.

He is checking out of the hotel at the foot of the mountain. The innkeeper has wire-frame glasses and ice-blue eyes. He has just told Anders that it is a shame he is leaving, since on top of the mountain is a temple in which lives the beautiful lady with the face of gold. The lady will free his conscience. He begins to climb the mountain. An old woman appears part way up, from behind a large rock, and follows him. When the crest comes into view, he finds only a forest of dead trees. Dark storm clouds boil above the trees. He is afraid, and his belly cramps. The old woman grabs his shoulder from behind. He turns, and her parchment-colored face breaks into a grimace. He realizes she is in league with the innkeeper. She begins shaking him. She demands to know where his daughter is.

Anders wakes in a sweat, with a bad headache. He is lying somewhere in darkness. The dream is familiar. Didn't he have a similar dream wake him this morning? Wasn't there the voice of San Bartolomeo trying to reassure him?

He hears strange noises. He listens. It must be Anna and Thomas making a ruckus. When he and Kate stay at La Lilia they always pay extra to have the children in a room next door.

"Kate?" The word comes out hoarsely. There is no answer. "Kate, the children must be up to something." There is no echo—the hotel must have found them a very small room. "Dear, shall I check on them?" He sighs. She has always been a heavy sleeper. He works himself upright, reaches out and finds the lamp switch. The room blazes into light. The colors, shapes

164

and edges of things hurt his eyes. Yes, the room is tiny. The hotel has put them in a maid's room this time. Outrageous. But where is Kate? She must have gone to check on the children.

His eyes play about the room. He is surprised to see a bottle of bourbon on the nightstand. Old Crow, two thirds full. He reaches up, takes the bottle, twists off the cap, and brings it to his nose. Would this help his headache? Probably not. What a sea of curious memories and illuminations erupt from that rich aroma—banks of clouds on fire from the desert's setting sun, yips of coyotes in the night, vivid faces of women whose names he has forgotten. How did this bourbon find its way here? He cannot recall ordering room service. How then? The answer seems lost down long passageways of memory too remote to pursue. He sets the bottle back on the nightstand, next to—he now notices—a file folder.

The folder now in his hands, he finds a calling card clipped to its cover. It is from a Doctor Giovanni Corsini. There is an address, also a telephone number. Inside the file he finds a sheet of the doctor's stationery with scribbled words, two of which are *commozione cerebrale*. Attached to the sheet is a chart with a graph and columns of numbers. It seems he has been taken to a hospital to be checked for a concussion. That explains the headache. So what happened? He can't tell. The important thing is that Kate and the children are next door. He must join them.

Fortunately he is fully clothed. He won't have to waste time dressing. He glances down at the cuffs of his shirt, his sweater, and his trousers. Yes, his jacket is draped over the back of the chair nearby. With effort he swings his legs over the edge of the bed and struggles to his feet. The action makes his head throb with pain. Putting his hand to his forehead he discovers a bandage above his eyes. It goes around his head and covers his temples. Has someone hit him? Has he been attacked? He tries to remember as he lurches toward the chair, his jacket, and his shoes.

Working his arms into his jacket's coarse sleeves, Anders hears a strange, high-pitched sound. It must be the children, acting up again. He must help Kate calm them. He sits down and pulls on his shoes.

The hallway is dark. He feels his way along the wall toward the strange sounds. He passes a closed door. The next door has light shining under it. He twists its knob and opens it.

A white-haired woman is crouching next to a tall, tripod-shaped device set up beside a bed. Somebody is in the bed. His mind swims. Where is he? Where are Kate and the children?

Is this old woman an ancient Sibyl, preparing to burn an offering to divine the will of the gods?

"*Professore?*"

It is the Sibyl, glancing up at him from her tripod. Will she speak of the underworld? No. She is preparing to insert a needle into the woman's arm. A bag with a clear liquid hanging from the tall tripod shakes slightly from her efforts. He notices a small clock on the bedside table, its hands indicating fifteen minutes past three—*in the morning?* Yes, the half-shaded window is dark. The Sibyl gazes at him as if waiting for an answer. She has the sort of worried smile a mother might have.

"*Sta bene, Professore?*" she asks.

Is he all right, he wonders? Hers is not just a customary greeting, but a sincere inquiry into his health. Yes, he is standing here, awake and perhaps not as strong as he once was. But what of this sick person? Is this one of his students—the loveliest one? But where are Kate and the children? He begins to shake from the terror of not knowing how to know.

"*Io sono Bianca...di ieri sera...*" the Sibyl says.

166

What does she mean by saying, "I am the Bianca of yesterday evening?" Was that when…when Kate said that the woman in this bed was his daughter? Did he imagine it? Collecting his thoughts, he puts his hand to his forehead. He rediscovers the bandage. Why a bandage? In any case, Kate is mistaken. This woman in the bed is not his daughter. Anna is where he left her in the *casita*. This Sibyl is acting as a nurse, tending to a patient. They are in a hospital, probably Santa Maria Nuova. He should have known that much from the file he found on his bed stand. He must tell her he understands.

"*Ho capito, grazie,*" he says.

"*Prego.*"

He should be familiar with the inside of Santa Maria Nuova, but he cannot recall the circumstances of his previous visit. He now finds himself staring at his upturned palms. Is he expecting to see blood? His heart is pounding. All will be well if he can find Kate and the children. He bows cordially and is about to leave, when the patient on the bed moans loudly. Something down a long corridor of memories begs for attention.

He asks the nurse if the patient is doing well.

"*Abbastanza bene, Professore.*"

Merely well enough? A fence-sitting sort of answer. One a logician, not a diviner, might deliver. He clears his throat and asks for the patient's name.

The nurse's expression is that of one who bears the weight of the world. "*Il suo nome e' Teresa, la povera.*" she says, her voice faltering.

"Teresa? Poor Teresa?" Named, he wonders, after which of two saints, the sixteenth-century Spanish Carmelite nun—or the beloved French Carmelite of the nineteenth century? He is beginning to sense an inexplicable connection with this patient who is doing well enough, though evidently not *so* well. As he stares at her, lying there, he feels an impulse to ask her for her blessing, for help in finding his little family. But would the white-haired nurse understand? Would she think he might be a threat to her patient? He tries to mentally assemble his entreaty…*Santa Teresa, tanto beata…*

"*Va a dormire di nuovo?*" It is the nurse. She is smiling anxiously at him.

No, he will not go back to sleep again, as she wants, but she must be made to think that he will. He points to the hands of the clock on the bed stand.

"*Sono stanco,*" he mumbles, to convince her that he is tired, will return to his room, and will trouble her no more. After all, the hospital may not want to discharge him yet and he has important work that will not wait. Kate and Thomas and Anna are expecting him, somewhere here in the city, perhaps at a kiosk on the Piazza della Repubblica. Or on the Ponte Vecchio where Kate might be lifting their children to watch the Arno's water surge underneath, as he himself has done many times.

But no, he thinks, glancing at the window's half-shaded darkness. They would not be at the kiosk, or on the Ponte Vecchio now. It is the middle of the night. The rain has stopped, but the wind still moans at the windows.

He gives the nurse and the figure in the bed a last look. "*Arrivederci, Santa Teresa,*" he murmurs. But as he turns to leave, the Saint gives a cry. It is a heart-wrenching cry, and Anders stops, as if she has cried to *him*. He turns back, takes the two steps to her bed, and lowers himself slowly to his knees. The Saint's swollen red hand lies near the edge of the bed. Before the nurse can stop him, he takes the precious red hand and gives it a long kiss. "*Ti amo tanto, Santa Teresa,*" he murmurs, pouring his love into the words. Yet he needs her blessing. *La vostra benedizione, per favore?*"

There is no answer from Santa Teresa. The nurse is at his side, helping him rise. She leads him to the door, closing it softly behind him. Yes, he tells himself, as he makes his way down the hallway, he has behaved humbly, begging the holy Santa Teresa for her help. Surely she will grant his wish. With her blessing he will find his young family.

Anders limps step by step down the dark narrow stairs, relying on his left leg and his hold on the railing. This must be the back stairwell used by the hospital staff, he thinks to himself. By the time he reaches the bottom of the steps he is frustrated and breathing hard. This kind of thing is dangerous. Hospitals have elevators, he knows, and he must find one. Feeling his way along the wall, it is dark, but he can tell by the echoes of his footsteps that he has entered a large chamber. He stumbles into a table, a chair, then another. Gratefully he lowers himself into one of the chairs.

Running his fingers along the chair's invisible curved arms, he is surprised at how luxuriously it is upholstered. As he settles himself into it, he wonders what kind of hospital this could be. It seems too silent, too unlit, and empty of patients and staff. There are no medicinal smells, no urine or antiseptic odors, not even the lingering scent of ammonia to clean the floor. Instead he notices mustiness and traces of cigarette smoke of the aromatic European variety. Then again, when he was recovering from the *autostrada* accident he remembers that Santa Maria Nuova had the feel of a medieval palazzo converted to medical purposes. He won't forget being unnerved by the sight of clouds of mosquitoes high in the hospital's vaults above him. Little had progressed in the way of medical hygiene, it seemed, since the 14th century.

He cocks his head now and listens. Did he just hear voices? He holds his breath and tries to hear into the darkness. Yes.

Now he hears voices again. They're coming from a room nearby. He doesn't want to be discovered, wandering around, a stranger. He struggles up out of the chair, and, moving carefully, approaches the room with the voices. The door is closed, but he can hear through it. One of the voices sounds familiar. Is it Kate's voice?

Anders can't stand it. He pulls the door open and steps inside. He gropes the wall until he finds the switch. In the flare of sudden light he can see that he is alone in an empty library, nobody there but books. A library in a hospital? Anders scratches his head. The patients and medical staff must be very well read. He stares at the two large windows at the far end. The wind outside is whistling, catching the sills and the panes, hissing, murmuring, whispering. That must have been what he heard, he realizes, not voices.

He must hurry. Kate and the children are expecting him. He turns off the light, leaves the room, and sets off again into the darkness of the galleries. Passing the dim outline of a heavily curtained window, he stops to push the fabric aside. Like the other *inginocchiate* windows, this one extends almost to the floor. He stares through the patterned glass at the distorted web of street lamps that stretch into the night. The headlights, then taillights of a car pass below. He stares at the broad shape of the river that flows below him like a channeled black sea. How different the Arno is at night, he thinks. Where are the sculls, the rowing shells that glide up and down the water's bright surface, the tanned rowers bending their backs as they pull on their oars? But no, it is all darkness. Somewhere out there, his family is waiting for him.

He turns away from the window. Favoring his right leg, feeling his way along the wall, he moves past a doorframe into another open area. He follows a wall, curving to the right, until he steps off into space, and nearly falls. It must be another staircase, he thinks, but these steps seem wide and deep, and the thick stone banister is cold to the touch. Taking one careful step at a time, he at last reaches the bottom of the curving stairs—and nearly falls under an assault of frantic, echoing barks. It must be a small dog, perhaps a spaniel.

"*Shhhhh—basta,*" he whispers authoritatively. "*Non abbaiare!* You'll wake everyone." The barking is replaced by whining. Anders instinctively reaches into his jacket pocket—for what? Was it only days ago that he gave one to—was it Cleopatra, in the desert? He pulls the biscuit from his pocket. Holding it on the tips of his fingers, Anders bends and carefully extends it down into the darkness.

"Here, my little guardian," he whispers. The whining stops, and Anders feels the biscuit being tugged from his fingers. He hears the sound of it being cracked and munched by sharp little teeth. He reaches out to stroke the invisible furry body.

"Are we alone, my friend? Where are all the patients? Sleeping? Or discharged, off with their lovers in the Italian fashion?"

With the pup bribed into at least temporary friendship, it is time to find the portal to the outside. Bumping against what feels like a pilaster, he gropes into the blacker darkness. Inching along, trying not to step on the dog's paws, he comes up against a wall of wood with metal fastenings. He's found a pair of massive doors. Propping himself against them, Anders runs his hands over the vertical surfaces until he feels a thick iron shaft, bolts and a lock. He guesses that the vertical shaft now under his fingers runs up into a hole in the stone lintel, locking the right-hand door into place. He is familiar with the system—it is similar to the doors on the Greve house.

His fingers detect the horizontal bar, held by iron brackets, that prevents the doors from opening. Bracing himself, he lifts the bar out of its brackets and sets it aside. His little friend is whimpering again, and Anders pauses to stroke him. "Sorry, *amico mio*," he whispers, "that was my only *biscotto*."

Reaching up, he grabs the knob on the end of the vertical bolt and pulls downward. It doesn't budge. Gasping from his efforts, he sinks to the floor where the dog is instantly on him, lapping at his face, squealing excitedly. He holds the animal close for a moment, quieting it, gathering his strength. He must hurry. Who knows who may have been roused by the commotion? He struggles to his feet, and as he reaches out for support, his hand brushes against a large key he missed in the darkness, hanging from an iron hook in the wall. He takes the key down, finds the lock, inserts it, and turns it with a loud click. He listens. Are those hurrying footsteps upstairs? He pulls the heavy door partly open and squeezes through. He closes it behind him, prompting a volley of barks.

Outside, he stumbles down the steps to the river's Lungarno walkway, with its lit streetlamps. The rain has stopped. He marvels at his escape. Even if he is not thinking clearly, some reliable part of him has risen to action. He begins a shambling, stuttering attempt at running. Does he hear the creak of doors opening behind him? Is someone calling? He turns the building's corner, stops and listens. Nothing. The night is cool and clear; the damp sidewalk shines dully. He looks upward and stares. Between patches of clouds floating high in the sky's black canopy are islands of tiny diamonds. The stars! *The stars!*

Chapter Fourteen

Anders takes a step, then another. There's still no sound of anyone following him. He starts off, quickly and clumsily, taking the Lungarno toward the Ponte Vecchio. The light from the walkway's tall street lamps, stretching far ahead, illuminates the bridges, making them appear ghostly. Where in this night landscape, he wonders, can he expect to find Kate and the children?

Within minutes he stops, confused. Unearthly noises, like the chattering of spirits, are rising from somewhere nearby. He edges toward the parapet, leans over, and peers down. Somewhere on the river's bank people are talking—men's and women's voices—but there is too little light to see who they might be. For a moment he imagines he might be listening to the chatter of the doomed, waiting to cross to the land of the dead. He strains in vain to decipher the conversation. No, his little family cannot be down *there*. He shakes his head, turns, and lurches off in the direction of the Ponte Vecchio. His bad foot is able to bear weight, yet it conveys little feel of the pavement underfoot.

The sky is giving its first hint of light in the east, beyond the church of Santa Croce. An occasional car or *motorino* grumbles awake in invisible parts of the city. He can begin to see human shapes crossing the Lungarno from the Via Por Santa

Maria. He must be cautious, move soundlessly. It is a time when thieves, hiding in shadows, wait for their victims. He puts his shaking hand to his forehead. There is the bandage again. Who put it there? Was it last night?

How could Kate have brought the children outside in *this?* Possible danger everywhere. He must get a grip on himself and quell a growing fever in his brain. There, ahead of him, its horizontal shape outlined against the night sky, is the massive span of the Ponte Vecchio. Yes, he remembers, instead of the *botteghe* of jewelers and goldsmiths it now houses, it once held shops of butchers who tossed slaughtered animals' bowels, hooves and skins into the fresh current below. Anders used to wonder how many assassins disposed of victims by mixing their dismembered remains with the entrails of hogs and cattle.

As he gets closer, he examines the span. Hidden below its roof, he knows, is the elevated corridor designed by Vasari for the old Medici rulers, should they need to escape assassins in the Palazzo Vecchio, so long the seat of government. Fortunate were those who could flee from the Palazzo through the Uffizi's east wing corridor, across the Ponte Vecchio to the Arno's south bank, to the Palazzo Pitti and safety. Anders shakes his head: where is *his* Vasari? Where is *his* escape corridor? But he is not escaping assassins—he has left them behind. He is searching for his family.

Reaching the north end of the old bridge, he peers across its length, the gloom lit faintly by its overhead lamps. He can make out sleeping shapes, some propped against the stonework, others lying flat as corpses. He takes a step back. Are a few of those shapes only pretending to sleep? Are some waiting for him with butcher's knives? What police would be on duty at this hour to hear a victim's cries? Before he can take an unsteady step, he feels a hand tug at his jacket. He whirls, almost falling, the hair rising on the back of his neck. An old woman is pulling at him—or an old man, he can't tell which. The cloak's hood has fallen over half the face, the rest in shadow.

"*Hai degli spiccioli?*"

Beggars everywhere, wanting spare change. Is she a Roma—a Gypsy? But her arms clutch no grimy infant. Her withered face, her hollow voice uttering the feeble syllables—all spook him, and he recoils, yanking his jacket from her bony fingers.

"*Va' via,*" he mutters. "Go away."

"*Per favore, signor…*" Her voice now sounds pitiful; her hand is extended, palm up, fingers crumpled inward, as if already cupping a tiny offering.

"I said, *va' via—sono occupato.* I'm busy. *Io cerco ancora la mia famiglia*—I'm searching for my family."

"*Ma io—io sono la vostra famiglia, signor.*"

What does she say? I am your family?

"*Posso aiutare…*"

She says she can help? He squints, trying to make out her features, trying to guess if he *does* know her. He decides she means only that he and she belong to the *human* family. He must be careful. Didn't the Roma once attack him in the Milano train station, using their sheets of cardboard to hide their thieving hands as they picked his pockets? "It's not true," he says, brushing her away. "*Va' via!*"

"*Vo' maledire,*" she says, shaking her fist.

She threatens to curse him? He tears himself away—he will not wait to hear. He starts across the bridge, glancing back to be sure she is not following. Yes, there she is, still shaking her upraised arm at him. He stops and stares. But could this be a Sibyl? Like the other one he encountered—the prophetic one? What if she *can* help find Kate and the children? He turns and walks back to her. She drops her arm, ceases her cursing, and is silent.

"*Hai il dono*—do you have the gift?" he asks, close enough to see a gleam in her eyes.

"Do you deserve its fruit?" she replies in guttural Italian.

"Fruit everywhere," he laments under his breath. "I will pay."

"Ah, *now* you have *denaro*." She turns half away.

"I need..."

"Ah, *now* you need," her voice rasps.

He feels her staring at him, the beak of her nose protruding like that of a bird of prey.

"I must find my wife and children. I will pay if you tell me where I can find them." He pulls coins from his pocket and holds them up to her face. "*Ecco qua*—two Euro pieces."

Her hand snakes out and the coins vanish. "Your family is there," she says, pointing past him. "*Sono là...nel Oltrarno*."

"Where? The other side?" He turns to look, as if he could see anything in the gloom that envelops the far side of the bridge. A pigeon flies from its roost overhead with a flapping whir of its wings. "*Where* across the river?" he asks.

"*Di là dal fiume*," she repeats, pointing. "Beyond! *La chiesa—San Miniato al Monte*."

"San Miniato?" he whispers, sensing a moment of clarity. "Above the Fourteen Stations of the Cross?"

"*Sì. Nel mondo dei morti*."

He gazes where she points. But she calls it the world of the dead. The Sibyl must have misunderstood. "But..." he begins.

"*Va' a trovare la vostra famiglia*," she mutters, waving him on.

She seems so certain, he thinks to himself. He makes his way to the midpoint of the ancient span. He stops and faces east, the upstream side. Lights are blinking on in buildings on both banks of the river as early-rising Florentines anticipate the dawn. Again, his eyes are drawn back to the Oltrarno end of the bridge, past the jewelry stores. Is the Sibyl trying to tell him that Kate and the children are in the underworld?

Fearful, Anders whirls to ask her again, but the Sibyl has disappeared. Can he trust her words? How could she think he would want the underworld? As he leans out over the inky water to better see the near buildings of the Oltrarno, one of the slumbering forms near his feet coughs.

"Don't do it, man." It is a voice at his feet. The accent is American—a young American.

"I can see you," Anders says, his breath coming fast. "I won't step on you."

"I mean—don't jump."

Anders had not thought to jump. "But if the Sibyl was right," he murmurs to himself, "this *would* be a way to find my family." He stares at the shapeless form at his feet. Again, he senses the beginnings of a headache. He reaches for his forehead and feels the bandage. What *does* it mean?

Anders smells the bridge's human residue: the faint odor of cigarettes and urine and unwashed bodies. "Why shouldn't I jump," he asks the young American, "if I have reason?"

"Life's awesome, man," the youth says. He moans, as if contradicting his own upbeat words, pulling himself to his knees and slumping against the wall. Anders makes out a white, oval face framed by long dark hair. Something drops away from the youth's hand or his clothing, clinking onto the stone, invisible in the shadows. The youth grubs around for it with both hands.

Awesome? It is a word Anders has come to despise, recalling the many times he has red-penciled it on term papers and exams. *Trivial tripe,* he would write, docking credit. Is it, he wonders, a word Thomas would use?

"Yeah, life's fucking incredible," the youth says, trying to pocket whatever it was that fell, catching it in the material of his jacket. "At night you hear the voices, everyone who ever crossed this bridge," he says in a monotone.

"Everyone, through the ages?" Anders asks skeptically.

"You know, there was this poet. Name of Dante. He used to stand at the end of this same bridge and watch for a girl. For a girl he, like, *craved*."

"Not this bridge. The Ponte Santa Trinita," Anders corrects. "Beatrice was her name. If he craved, it would have been her love he craved."

"Is that her name? Ouch!" The young man is still fussing with whatever it was he dropped and retrieved.

Anders wonders what it is. Money? Jewelry he's stolen? "She was the inspiration for his poetry."

"So, you see?"

"What?" Anders asks.

"Dante never let her get to him so bad he had to jump," the youth says dreamily. "He had poetry to write."

Anders' headache is becoming more insistent. "True. But remember that when you are old and alone, your search is for lost loved ones. And that is a different matter."

The youth is very close, and as he stares upward he fondles what Anders makes out to be a syringe, its needle gleaming. "Man, I know…" The youth's words are lost in a coughing fit.

Anders is suddenly riveted by the idea that here, not two feet away, is a young drug addict, like his Thomas. Anders peers down at him. "What keeps you on this bridge, young man?"

"Do you want to cross over to *that* side?" He raises his arm and points toward the Oltrarno.

The youth twists his head and presses his temple against the stone, his hands still caressing the syringe. "I guess you only go there if you know somebody. I don't know anybody over there."

"I do. I know somebody. The Sibyl says my family is there. She calls it the world of the dead. I think she misunderstood me."

The youth shrugs. "I thought you were going to find your family in the river."

Did he say that? "No," he says vacantly, "the Sibyl convinced me otherwise."

"You're confusing me. Did you fall and hit your head, sir?" His words come slowly and sleepily. "That looks like a bandage on your head."

Anders is startled. Do they all know about the bandage—the shame? But the youth has just addressed him as "Sir." On this Florentine bridge at what seems like the end of time, this note of respect is comforting. Like the caring touch of a parent, or a lover. The young man, he realizes, is in harm's way. With a swoop he grabs for the syringe, sticking himself as he wrests it away. With a flick he tosses it over the parapet and into the river. "Better it than you," he declares.

"But I wasn't going to. *You* were going to. Damn, that cost me." The youth tries to rise but is unable to.

"All I stole was your death," Anders whispers.

"It's the old woman. She told you stuff. She's just a beggar who doesn't know anything." He laughs hoarsely. "I can always get another one."

"I suppose so." Anders says, as if to anyone within hearing. He shuffles to the center of the bridge and peers back at where he'd come from, toward where the Sibyl disappeared. A shape is standing there by the parapet. Is she staring at him? He shudders.

He limps back past the youth and toward the Oltrarno, past the shuttered goldsmith and jewelry *botteghe*—the old butchers' shops in a previous age. He turns and calls back to the youth, "Remember this bridge when you're old, and remember me."

Leaving the bridge behind, he gazes down the Via de' Bardi, past the Lungarno Torrigiani and the Lungarno Serristori, past the distant hills at a sky glowing from a yet unseen sun. He shivers as a breeze blows in his face from upriver.

With his left hand, Anders pulls his jacket tight against the chill. He could use a hot *caffè*. He imagines it, concentrated and strong. His heart leaps. Is there an espresso bar nearby? He used to go and sip one while waiting for Kate to finish shopping with the children. Sometimes they took a long time. Is it possible? No. They would not be shopping before dawn. No espresso bar would be open. He glances behind him. Did he see a shadow move? Is someone following him? The youth? The Sibyl?

He hobbles off down the Via de' Bardi, checking behind him every dozen steps or so. A number of human shapes have already begun appearing in the gloom, approaching and passing him. Are they Florentines off to work, or to Mass? Or are they those without the concerns of the living? They are silent, these figures moving through the morning twilight. Some whisper to each other—about him? Two well-dressed women approach and pass, walking quickly and smartly, as Florentine ladies do. But he hears the lilt of Asian words. Was that Korean? He isn't sure, since he hasn't heard *that* language in so many years. Can he conjure a greeting before they're out of earshot?

"*Ahn-nyung-ha-sib-ni-ka,*" he calls after them, trying to pronounce the syllables in the polite form he recalls for "Hello—how are you?"

The women stop and turn. "*Non siamo Coreane,*" one says. "*Siamo Cinesi.*" He approaches them. Only now does he recall Sebastiano explaining that the Chinese work in the Florentine leather factories. The closer he gets, the more he is fascinated by what he can barely see, in the dim light, of the one who has not spoken.

"Ah," he says, "Chinese. Of course. The Korean language is more explosive. And here I thought I might know you charming ladies." They are eying him uncertainly. It is no doubt the bandage they are staring at, but his tweed jacket and polite demeanor should reassure them that he is no vagabond accosting them for spare change. Do Asians still respect age, as Westerners no longer do? "One of you reminds me of a special Korean lady whom I taught to love *La Divina Commedia*," he says in Italian.

"And so, you want to teach *us* also?" says the one who was silent, her tone ironic.

Her features appear luminous in the dimly dawning light, and he is struck by a resemblance to Miss Kim beyond the physical—a hint of teasing beneath her serenity. He feels faint, as if the woman he once loved is standing before him. He tries to speak, but he is consumed with a wave of guilt. As if the presence of this young woman is a deadly rebuke. Will she at any moment ask him, *"Why did you abandon me, my Dante?"*

"But perhaps you are too old to teach us," the teasing second one says, shyly.

Weak with emotion, he barely gets the words out. "I teach the work of Dante Alighieri. I am . . . I am Professor Anders Croft."

"We are in a hurry, *Professore*," says the first. "We are on our way to work, even on a Sunday. But we will remember you, and if we decide..."

"But my good ladies," he begins, his voice catching in his throat. Does he suddenly fear less for *his* safety than for *theirs*? Is he trying to correct past error, trying to rescue someone he neglected to save? He glances up and down the Via de' Bardi.

"This is a dangerous place before dawn, this Oltrarno. *Tanto pericoloso*—you do understand, don't you?"

They seem alarmed and take two steps back. "This is not a dangerous place," says the first one. "We *left* a dangerous place, where we are from, our village in China." They linger, uncertain.

"You must understand. I fear for you. I will be your guide to safety."

"We don't need a guide," says the first one.

"And your Korean lady?" It is the teasing, quiet one. "Where is she now?"

He points at the shadowy buildings nearby. "There. You see," he whispers, "this is the land where the lost lose themselves."

Glancing at each other, the young Chinese women seem to make up their minds. They walk away with quick, small steps.

"*Attenzione!*" he bellows hoarsely. "*Attenzione,* this part of town—it is *pericoloso*—dangerous." But there is no indication that the ladies have heard him. They must believe that *he* is the danger. Their footsteps recede toward the long dim silhouette of the Ponte Vecchio he just left. He tried. He is too late. He shuffles slowly eastward, toward the Via di San Niccolò, from which he will begin the long climb to the church of San Miniato al Monte.

Weary, his head throbbing from his wound, he deciphers the shape of a bench not far off, in a small open place away from the street. Favoring his right leg, aching by now, he makes it to the empty bench. Gently he lowers himself onto the smooth stone, groaning in relief. His mind relaxes its shaky grip on past and present. Seeing the Chinese ladies has pained him. His heart aches for his Miss Kim for the first time in years. Her sweet face lit by her quick bright spirit floats before him. He closes his eyes. He did not save her. But he will save his wife and children. First he must rest.

Chapter Fifteen

Anders awakens with a start. Stiff and cold, his spine aches from the hardness of the bench. The sun is rising in the east, its light already glittering on the distant river's rippling surface. He has just dreamed of Kate. He was calling to her across a dark body of water in the teeth of a gusting night wind. "Where are the children?" he shouted. "Are they with you?" But her answering calls were in an ancient language he could not understand. Or perhaps it was only the howling of the wind that he mistook for her voice.

Anders rubs his eyes, still emerging from his dream fog. He feels the bandage on his head and remembers that it was there before, but not why. Glancing around, he is startled to see a cloaked figure sitting at the other end of his bench. The figure turns toward him. It is an old woman. He has seen her before. She is the Sibyl.

"*Spiccioli, per favore?*" Her voice sounds too loud in the silence of the early morning. She holds a wavering hand out to him, palm open.

Didn't he give her something before? "I gave you more than pocket change. I gave you *Euros.*" He cannot remember how many. "Maybe six."

"Less." She turns away. "Four more and I will be your guide," she says, "*la vostra guida.*"

He collects his thoughts. The Sibyl has been following him. Is she more than just a pest? Can she really help him find Kate and the children? "How do you know where I need to go?" he asks in Italian.

"You want to find your family. You told me," she says. She points toward the mountain behind them. "We will climb the steps. They will lead us to the church, San Miniato. There we will find your family. Only I know where they are—*soltanto io.*"

Yes, she mentioned it before—the Stations of the Cross, the stepped path to San Miniato, a church Dante knew. "How do you know my family will be there?" Anders asks, peering at her, trying to decipher her intentions through the gloom.

"As you asked before, *io ho un dono di natura.*"

"I remember," he says. "You have the gift." The Sibyl he saw with Santa Teresa only hours ago—is this the same one? Has she already led Kate and the children safely up to San Miniato to pray to St. Minias?

His mind shunts off to the Florence of fifty years ago. He and Kate had decided one autumn afternoon to see the famous San Miniato church. Climbing terrace after terrace up the tall hill, the footpath finally crossed a paved road provided for motor traffic. Out of nowhere, a lumbering bus, blasting its horn as it rounded a curve, nearly hit them. When they reached the church, Kate decided to give thanks to St. Minias for saving them. Inside, she disappeared behind the altar into a small primitive chapel. He followed her, the chill of the trapped air and the smell of the ancient stone spooking him as he watched her pray to the Christian martyr who was beheaded in Roman times. Yes, Kate *would* return there in a time of need, wouldn't she? Might she be praying right now, he wonders, for his return?

The Sibyl has her hand out, still demanding her money. He

would pay a thousand Euros to see Kate and the children. He reaches into his pocket and pulls out coins. He selects his last two 2-Euro coins bearing the relief of the poet, and hands them to her.

"*Bene,* let us go" she says, as the coins disappear into the folds of her robe. She rises and sets off down the Via de' Bardi in a series of scuttling, crab-like movements, glancing at him over her shoulder.

He raises himself to his feet, his spine stiff as wood, and totters after her, favoring his right leg always. They soon pass the Palazzo Mozzi with its huge arched windows—dark, baleful cavities in the rough-hewn stone whose glass has begun to glow opaquely with the onset of the new day. If there are spirits behind those stark, staring windows, they are the ghosts of the powerful medieval Mozzi bankers.

Following the Sibyl onto the Via di San Niccolò, a huge city bus roars past, only feet away, jogging Anders' memory of another bus's long ago miss, and Kate's startled cry. His dream returns in fragments—his cries to Kate across the river, the water rising and widening, the wind stealing the sound of their voices. Why didn't he swim across to her?

"Professors weren't meant to be heroes," he mutters to himself. "And I'll see her soon."

The Sibyl is calling to him. She stands in the shadow of a building as if to escape the sun that is emerging now from behind the mountains. Anders limps after her. They soon pass a building where a piece of *graffiti,* a diagram of some kind, has been scrawled in black chalk on the stucco. He stops to examine it in the early morning light. It is a kind of crude circular mandala. The curving arrow at the top points from "Coca-Cola," to "uccide"—"Coca Cola kills." The bottom arrow completes the cycle, pointing from "uccide" to Coca-Cola—"Kill Coca Cola."

Anders squints, trying to make sense of it. Why Coca Cola, the banal sugary drink? But the longer he studies it, the more he understands its sinister message: Coca Cola is a stand-in for America.

Anders' stomach turns. Is his Americanism written all over him? The zealous graffiti artist would not know of Professor Croft's sympathy with much anti-American sentiment. How unfair that the Florentine *communista* does not know this. He limps on after the Sibyl, turning the molten question over in his mind: "*America kills, kill the American.*"

As he passes the Church of San Niccolò Oltrarno, Anders glances over his shoulder. Far back, a man has paused in the shadow of a doorway on the street he has just left. Anders follows the Sibyl for a few seconds, and again looks back. The man has stopped to examine the wall with the *graffiti* mandala. He has on dark glasses and is wearing a black felt fedora of a kind that was stylish generations ago. He has what appears to be a black cape over his shoulders. An ivory-colored scarf covers his neck and lower face. The effect is ominous. He is the image of a Sicilian godfather.

Is the man really interested in the drawing, or only pretending to be? Does he know the *graffiti* perpetrator? And those theatrical clothes—is this what Death chooses to wear when he confers the final kiss? Could he be one of the devious guests— it comes back to him now—from the dinner he attended last night? Could he be a crafty lawyer with a goatee? Could he be a clever doctor with soaring temples and a widow's peak, pretending to admire his own scribbled handiwork?

Anders' mind releases itself like an unclenching fist, caving in to the terror of this Sicilian godfather, or whoever he is. As he walks, Anders peers furtively behind him. His pursuer is strolling blithely, as if it is a sunny day in the country. He glances this way and that, keeping a modest distance. How perfectly he calibrates his presence, Anders thinks, as he takes another unsteady step, and stops.

What if he is not being followed for the crime of being an American? What if he is being followed for some other reason? He would readily admit his weakness for women in a court of justice— admit his love for Niven, for Miss Kim, and for the others. They did not die by his hand, yet they were under his protection. God must see that he mourns them.

Overwhelmed by weariness, he is too weak to slam the door on the voices and images spilling into his mind. He staggers and leans for support against a wall of the Church of San Niccolò Oltrarno. He wishes he could climb into its belfry and hide. Michelangelo once hid in that same belfry, afraid of being executed by an invading French army for having designed Florence's defenses against them. Could he claim similar reprieve?

The Sibyl has stopped and is staring back at him. She would not fathom why finding Kate and the children will set everything right. Anders peers back over his shoulder. The Godfather has stopped, keeping his distance. He will give his quarry no chance to explain his excellent political credentials. Is that his point—to prevent the unfortunate Dr. Croft from proving his innocence? For God's sakes, why does the man hang back? Why can't he *confront* his victim? It is terrifying, this ragged march, this lockstep toward the ancient city wall, toward the Fourteen Stations of the Cross.

Chapter Sixteen

A nders watches, ahead, as the Sibyl now passes through the great Gate. She turns and stares back at him. Why is her expression so stern? He is distracted by two sparrows, darting overhead, their flight paths interweaving with lightning speed. They are full of life, soaring, while he is not. Would it be unseemly for him to spare a tear for himself? Obediently, he follows the Sibyl through the Gate. They are leaving Florence and its towering city wall behind them.

But he is struck by a thought. What of Santa Teresa in the hospital? Who is caring for *her*? He stumbles forward and catches up to the Sibyl. He grabs at her sleeve. "*E Santa Teresa, per favore?*" he pleads. "Have we abandoned her?"

She stares at him over her shoulder, and by the light of dawn her features appear chiseled in stone. The hawk nose, the shriveled lips, and the deep-set sunken eyes seem to skewer him with a strange distaste. "*Non lo so,*" she replies, pulling away to continue her stuttering, sideways ascent.

"She doesn't know?" Anders mumbles to himself as he limps after her. "If *she* doesn't know, who does?" Who would abandon a saint to the mercy of others? She might be choking, unable to breathe, no one to save her.

He stops still. Is that why the Sibyl gave him that look of distaste? She knows past as well as future? Could she have seen what happened to those he didn't save? It is one more reason to find Kate, to justify himself in the eyes of both Kate and the Sibyl. What a blessing it will be to see his wife's glowing eyes, to have their light replace the Sibyl's stare of disdain.

Anders glances up at the ancient wall of stone blocks that runs along the road's right side, a wall so high it dwarfs the buildings nearby. Tufts of grass and weeds protrude from its niches like hair sprouting from an old man's ears. He suddenly wishes he were up there with the lizards, sluggish in the morning chill, lying out of reach, hidden in cracks along the top tier of stones.

Glancing back, Anders sees the man so like a Godfather hurrying up the rise, his fedora pulled low, his dark glasses impenetrable. Are those black lenses meant to speak for the blindness of Justice, the Lady who cannot be bought—or seduced? Anders raises his hand to his forehead to wipe away the sweat. Again there is that strange bandage.

Ahead, his clairvoyant guide has passed a parked blue car and a row of chain-bearing concrete posts. She is climbing the first stone steps of the Stations of the Cross. He follows her lead. The steps are long and flat, spaced so far apart that a climbing rhythm is difficult. He stops to catch his breath. To his right, crosses and cypresses march along, one after another, rising into the upper shadows.

On his left runs an ivy-covered wall, dark green vegetation billowing high over its top. He comes to a plaque of white marble set into the wall, partly hidden by the branches. Anders limps near and peers up at it. Engraved are words from the *Purgatorio*, written by Dante when he was in exile in Ravenna. The poet remembers the carved-rock steps leading up to the hilltop Church of San Miniato, with its view of his beloved Florence. He would never see his city again.

A woman and a boy brush past him. The boy is pushing a

bicycle toward the steps. Anders gasps. Is he mistaken? The woman looks just like the one who owns the *salumeria* not far from the Duomo. And isn't that her son, who was struck while riding his bicycle? Is the Sibyl right? Can this be the world of the dead?

Before he can be sure that it is the same mother and the son, Anders notices two young priests in black cassocks, perhaps seminarians, descending the steps toward him. They are speaking to each other in low tones. He reaches out, on impulse, to touch the sleeve of the nearest, as if for a benediction. Surely, they will understand. If they will only pause to learn of his mission—to find the beautiful, dark-haired American woman with whom he long ago exchanged sacred vows. They will understand his misery at his long separation from her.

But the young seminarians pass, absorbed in their world. He could not tell if they were discussing Augustine, Aquinas—or even which of the sports clubs will win this year. With them goes his fleeting fantasy of absolution...though in any case he is no Catholic. He watches them descend the steps, down to where the blue car is parked. There, standing by the concrete posts, his fedora pulled low, his scarf wrapped tight, is the Godfather. He seems to be pretending, like a tourist, to gaze out over Florence's sea of red tile rooftops.

With an involuntary grunt Anders turns and starts up the steps. Will he reach Kate and Anna and Thomas before it is too late? The Godfather assassin may try to catch him alone, without witnesses. Ahead, the Sibyl is almost out of sight, disappearing into the shadows above. Anders struggles to catch up. He limps past the high Crosses and the cypresses that march upward beside the stone steps, one after another, as far as he can see.

He is about to pause for breath when a group of eight or nine tourists overtakes him. One of them brushes by Anders, knocking him off balance. He stumbles, barely catching the nearest cross, wrapping his arms around its shaft midway between its stone base and high transom. Holding on with all his strength, he watches the group follow the leader up the steps above him.

But *what evil is this?* The black-caped figure with the fedora and white scarf—the Godfather—is *among* them. He has passed him! Will this Mafioso kill him before he can find his family?

"Stiffen your spine, Croft," he mutters to himself. "You're a *man*, for God's sake. You *will* find your wife and children." The tourists and the Godfather are almost out of sight. In their wake stands the Sibyl, staring down at him. Maybe she is finally tired, he thinks to himself. He releases the cross, kisses it, and limps up the stone steps toward her. He needs her good will now more than ever. "*Come stai, cara?* Are you well, dear one?" he yells hoarsely. "Are you tiring yourself?"

"*Mai,*" she answers. "Never. I am fine. *You* are not so fine. Come, move yourself." Her tone is gruff and unyielding.

Anders focuses all his strength on mounting each new step, fixing his eyes on his guide as if she is a beacon in a storm. The cypress branches converge overhead here, creating a deepening tunnel. Who is this Sibyl he trusts to lead him? What if she betrays him? Worst, as he struggles to close the distance between them, he feels heavy with a different doubt: does he even deserve to regain Kate and his children, to hug and kiss them?

"But I never raised a hand against those I adored," Anders mumbles as if to an inquisitor, lengthening his wobbly stride. "I loved them too much to hurt them," he murmurs. "I suppose I did not always behave as if I loved them. Yet someone," he says, raising his eyes to the sky above the heavy cypress branches, "may have noticed my saving that boy on the Ponte Vecchio. It wasn't much, but might I be considered for that small act of mercy?"

As he asks the question, a clear treble voice in front of him asks, "*Possiamo*...May we pass?"

Anders stands aside to allow a young couple, obviously just married, to descend the steps. The blonde bride, in her snowy bridal gown, her cheeks flushed, is a living vision of Botticelli's *Primavera*. The young, aquiline-nosed groom, with his dark curly hair, resplendent in his morning coat, smiles proudly. It is an apparition from another time, another place. Yes, he recalls, some of the couples, after being married in San Miniato or San Salvatore, visit the Piazzale Michelangelo to watch the rays of the rising sun bathe the awakening city. Afterwards they descend the Stations of the Cross to joyfully re-enter Florence, united as one.

As Anders watches the couple pass, he feels a shiver of joy. Didn't he and the young Kate Summers, years ago, enter a new world that way, all of life before them? Didn't they have dreams of their life together, he as a university professor and she as a concert pianist? And wouldn't there be children—wonderful children? He will be reminding her of those days soon, perhaps in minutes.

But what is this? Someone ahead is waving at him—the Sibyl? Far up the steps, in the shadows of the cypresses, she wants him to hurry.

Trying vainly to run, dizzy and gasping for air, he finally reaches her. They are near the top, where bushes and hedges form green by-ways that shield lovers from prying eyes. He hears the early Sunday morning traffic above—the cars and buses on the Viale Galileo Galilei that passes in front of the church of San Miniato. But here, below, the Sibyl is pointing at a gap in a hedge.

"*Va' a trovare*—go find your family," she says sternly.

He peers at where she is pointing, but he sees no Kate, no children, only thick hedges under green-leafed trees. "Where?" he asks, out of breath and confused. "*Ma dove?*"

"*There,*" she repeats. But she has also turned her palm upward. "*Denaro...soldi*—now you pay me."

"Again?" It seems sheer theft. Yet if Kate and the children are really yards away, waiting beyond the hedges? "*Sicuro?* Are you sure they're there?"

The Sibyl nods vigorously. "*Sicuro.*"

With a grunt Anders pulls bills from his pocket. Shakily he peels off a 10-Euro note and slips it into her outstretched palm. "*Grazie!*"

"*Prego!*" she answers, tucking the bill away.

Anders watches her scuttle away. She glances back at him every few steps until she disappears into the lower shadows. If his family is nearby, he knows, the old one has been a godsend, his 10 Euros a pittance.

He turns to examine the hedges. "Kate?" he calls. "Anna? Thomas?" There is only silence. Suspicious but hopeful, he makes his way through the foliage, brushing past the small sharp branches. "Kate? Are you here?" He finds an opening in a second hedge and pushes through, into a small grassy space. There to his horror, not twelve feet away, his back turned, his black-caped shoulders heaving, is the Godfather. On the grass by his shoes lie the heaped white scarf, fedora, and the sunglasses.

"*Finalmente, Professore,*" his tormentor says without turning around. "You look for the wife who died through your negligence? And the dead son you abandoned? And a daughter you left in the belly of a young girl, when you ran away?"

The voice is weirdly familiar. Anders can't believe his ears. This is no murderous Mafia assassin come to kill him. This is...

"I, too, search," the man continues, "but for the *respect* I deserve, which you violated as surely as you seduced the cousin I loved, saddling her with a crippled daughter, shaming my family."

Anders stares, disbelieving. It is Sebastiano who whirls to face him. His Cardinal-of-the-Church wire-rim spectacles have now replaced the dark glasses. His face is pale and distorted with rage, his shoulders are heaving, his body shaking. What is he saying? It doesn't matter—it is a huge relief to see the concierge, his friend. "Sebastiano! Thank God it's you! The Sibyl has found you, brought me to you!"

"As I paid her to. But you—look at *you! Che disgrazia!*" the concierge hisses.

"Sebastiano, what's the matter? Why am I a disgrace? Are you all right?"

The concierge takes a step forward and stops, his face suddenly crimson. "Why did you return to Florence? Why do you make me do this—I, the only one who can avenge poor Teresa, the only one who can reclaim the respect of my family? Do you understand, American?"

Anders takes a step back. The concierge has clearly lost his mind. "But I still love Diana, as *you* do. I am shocked to discover I have a daughter so...so..."

"So mutilated." The concierge grins horribly, his mouth stretched into a rictus. "Yes, *mutilata*. And I am the little epileptic Sebastiano who harms nobody, who makes restaurant reservations for hotel guests, who attends opera every week, who does not drive, cannot live, because he is cursed by God to live a shadow life, like Teresa. But now I challenge all of that. It is time."

Anders is paralyzed, speechless. Sebastiano is like an Inferno demon, glowering at him, unrecognizable, a maniac.

"Yes, *Professore,* I always wondered how it would feel to be Tosca when she won vengeance…when she stabbed the monster Scarpia in the Second Act…when she came at him, screaming '*Questo è il bacio di Tosca*—This, *this* is the kiss of Tosca!'"

Anders staggers backward. "Sebastiano, old friend…"

"*This* is the kiss of Sebastiano—the kiss of my family!"

As if in a dream, Anders watches the concierge pull something gleaming out of his waistband and fly at him, punch him in the stomach once, twice, his eyes round and staring behind the wire-rimmed lenses, his lips wet with saliva. But now the concierge staggers back, collapses slowly to the ground, his body stiffening, convulsing, the hand that held the fallen knife turned into a claw raking at the grass, his mouth making hideous croaking sounds.

Anders turns slowly away, his hand going to his stomach. The concierge did not really stab him, did he? He only punched him. Why? The poor concierge is having one of his fits. Too much stress. Good of Sebastiano not to stab him, instead he only punched him. But Anders brings his hand up, and it is covered with blood. It didn't feel like a knife stab. Only like a hard punch—two hard punches…so how did this happen?

He must find Kate and the children. They will be worried, he has been away so long. He cannot remember telling them where he would be—off to buy a *Herald Tribune* or a copy of *La Nazione*? Perhaps the dream—will San Bartolomeo help him? Or Santa Teresa? *Somebody?*

Anders hears the sound of traffic, of cars and buses, the putter of a motorbike. Not far off, church bells have begun to ring. He pushes through the hedges toward the sounds, his blood-wet hand pressed flat and protective against his stomach. He falls down, regains his feet and falls again, tripping over unseen obstacles. His stomach has begun to ache—sharply and badly.

He bursts through the foliage and finds himself on the edge of the Viale, where the cars and the buses appear out of nowhere, passing both from the left and the right. He begins to limp along the verge, toward the right, toward...he forgets. He understands only the direction. A careening car barely misses him, blowing its horn.

After walking for what seems a terribly long time he sees the chalk-white marble steps and marble balustrades on the opposite side of the road. A miracle. It is La Chiesa—San Miniato— where Kate and the children must be waiting for him. There is no organ music this time, no Bach Fugue, only bells, the cathedral's bells that are ringing. The Sibyl was right. She knew. And there! In the flash between a bus and a car—he can barely restrain his joy—there they are! Standing among others on the steps are Kate, and Anna, and little Thomas. *They waited—they did not give up!* Do they see him? He can't be sure, with the traffic. Yes, little Thomas seems to see him. He is pointing in Anders' direction, now pulling at Kate's hand, trying to get her attention.

He takes a delirious step toward his family, then another, crossing the road, the bus a mere phantom, so that when the impact sends him flying toward his family through the air of clanging bells, all other sensation fleeing his body, he is like a dandelion puff, the feathery seeds blowing to the corners of the universe, all noise ebbing.

Chapter Seventeen

(Three days later)

For the second time, Anna opens her purse and checks herself in her mirror. As usual, her curly, cinnamon-colored hair won't behave—she hasn't been able to properly wash it—and her face is blotchy and red from stress. She has even cried. Did Anders really mean that much to her, the father who wasn't? Perhaps he meant more than she thought. She slips the mirror back into her purse and snaps it closed. She glances around the huge room, which is like something out of a museum or a history book. The parquet floor, the drapes, the maroon brocade walls, the tapestries, even the table in front of her, its surface set with gem-like stones, seem fit for a fairy tale. Who could live like this? Only European aristocrats, apparently. And who is this Contessa di San Giorgio? She owns the La Lilia hotel, but how did she know Anders? Was he such a good customer over the years that the Contessa feels obliged to express her condolences? Is she so obliged that she doesn't bill his daughter for her elegant hotel room with its stunning view over the Florentine red-tile rooftops? Were they friends in the old days, the Contessa a friend of her mother's, too? The questions go around and around in her head as she wonders why the woman is keeping her waiting. Didn't the butler, or whoever he was, tell her that she was here?

Anna's thoughts bend back to Arizona: are Katey and Tommy all right? She calculates the time difference in her head. She'll phone them at four this afternoon to catch them before they go off to school. When the Italian Consulate called on Sunday with the news, she didn't know anybody in Tucson she could have left them with. She prays that Miranda is responsible. Anders wouldn't have hired her unless she *was* responsible, would he? Unless of course, as in the old days, responsibility took a back seat to a housekeeper's allure—and Miranda Lopez is not unattractive. But Tommy and Katey's mummy will be back in a few days, as soon as she decides whether to ship Anders' remains home or bury him next to her mother, here in Italy (she found nothing in the will about wanting either burial or cremation). She hears the rapid click of approaching heels on the hard parquet floor.

"*Mi dispiace,* Anna," says a lady in her mid-forties, approaching in black slacks and gray sweater, a string of bright pearls at her throat. Her silver-streaked blonde hair is pulled back, her head is tipped to the side, her arms extended. Her dark eyebrows lift over luminous gray eyes filled with compassion. "Please forgive me," the Contessa says, "it is our *maggiordomo* Giacomo's day off, and my husband forgot to tell me that you had arrived. Anna, I am so sorry about your father."

Anna rises to greet her, relieved that the Contessa speaks English, the little Italian she knew as a child long forgotten. She hesitates before taking the Contessa's outstretched hands. "Thank-you for your kindness, but please don't worry…" she begins, uncertain what to say. She feels awkward in these surroundings, an awkwardness compounded by her confused feelings about Anders and his death. After all, she felt she lost him years ago, when she was a little girl, when his warmth toward her turned strangely cold. It has been only a few weeks since she fled to his desert *casita* out of desperation, emotionally roiled as she was by her decision to take the children, leaving Sanderson and her broken marriage. Where else could she go on such short notice? Besides, something in her was determined to finally confront the man who seemed at the heart of her inability to trust or feel accepted by *any* man. She considered his sudden fleeing to Italy—fleeing *her*, unwilling to face her—a cowardly act. And yet, what are these pangs of guilt she is feeling? If she hadn't arrived on his doorstep a month ago wouldn't he now be alive in his desert *casita*? How can she begin to explain such a constellation of resentments and regrets, now, to an Italian stranger who must be expecting her to mourn her supposed father unreservedly?

"You see, Anders and I were not close. Though this is all so unexpected," Anna adds. "It brings back my mother's death in a way I couldn't have anticipated. The time I received the news that she was dead...I remember the name of the man who told me, when I was a little girl. It was a Mr. Donati. The accent of the man at the Italian Consulate last Sunday night reminded me of that day." Anna stops, her own voice echoing in her ears. What has she just said? Is she running off at the mouth, being too personal with a stranger? She has always prided herself on being tough and self-possessed, but now she senses her inadequacy, a kind of mental slippage. "Thank-you, Contessa, for not charging me for my lovely room at the hotel. That is very kind of you."

"Oh, Anna, please call me Diana. The least I can do is make your stay here in Florence a bit more bearable. Giving you a room is my pleasure. You see, I feel I owe much to your father," she says, "as well as to your mother."

"To my mother, too?"

"Yes, to your mother, too. I always felt guilty that it was

199

in our lovely city that her life was cut short." The Contessa's voice has faded as she speaks, her eyes heavy-lidded, as if she is suddenly absent. But she seems to recover her composure. "You spoke of Mr. Donati, who told you about your parents' accident so many years ago. He is my cousin, you see." Anna can see tears coming to the older woman's eyes. "Sebastiano Donati is the concierge at La Lilia, where you are staying. He is in the hospital just now. The seizure he suffered was an especially bad one. He is epileptic. This time he is unable to speak. The doctors say he had a stroke."

"Your cousin?" Anna summons a fuzzy picture of Mr. Donati's face after all these years—a receding hairline, steel-rimmed spectacles—as she tries to put together the pieces of what the Contessa is saying. What *is* this Florentine family? Who are these people who seem so involved with the deaths of Anders and her mother? She releases Diana's hands and takes a step back, nearly stumbling. She collects herself. "I'm so sorry about Mr. Donati." What else can she say? "You and your cousin—I mean, Anders *would* have friends here in Florence, wouldn't he, coming back all these years later to a city so important to him?" Yes, the life Anders had, a life she knew little of.

"*Cara* Anna, please be comfortable. Let's sit down. Your nerves must be worn thin. Let me get you a glass of wine, or a Campari. But have you had lunch? Would you like something to eat?"

Anna wonders if her own nerves are affecting this Contessa. "I have not, no, but honestly, I'm not hungry. I've barely eaten since yesterday, when I had to view Anders' body to identify him. It was difficult." She will not forget his face, bruised and bluish, like a badly sculptured facsimile of him, the rest of his body covered. "I couldn't bear to look at him for more than a second. He was with us in Tucson only last

Thursday." She glances at the nearby window, at the bright sun shining through the leaded glass.

Diana smiles sympathetically. "Well, what are your plans, now, Anna?"

"Tomorrow morning I'm going to rent a car and drive to Greve in Chianti, to the cemetery to visit my mother's grave. We lived there as a family once. Of course, you must know that. I'll have to decide whether to bury him alongside her." She turns to Diana. "But what I don't understand is, exactly how did he die? The police say they are still investigating and won't tell me much. They talked about—do you know anything about a knife wound?"

Diana gazes at Anna for a long moment. "Ah, *cara*, it is all so complicated, and it is so sad for you. I will explain, but again, would you care for a glass of wine? I think we both might need it."

Anna, her question turned aside, nevertheless agrees, and watches Diana disappear into the next room. She surveys her surroundings—the museum-like furniture, the tapestries, the painted frescoes high above. She is struck dizzy by the extent to which Anders was a stranger to her, the way he existed in a world alien to the world she knew, with his incomprehensible friends and acquaintances, and his agendas. She surely should bury him in this strange land, where he belongs.

Diana returns minutes later carrying a tray with a bottle of wine, two glasses, a dish with wedges of cheese and thin slices of bread. Anna watches her set the tray on the table, mildly surprised by the Contessa's expertise at performing a mundane task that a servant would have performed had it not been his day off.

"*Per favore,* please join me here on the couch," Diana says as she sets out plates and napkins, then transfers the wine, cheese and bread from the tray. "Do you find it chilly in here?" She glances around the room, hugging herself for a second. "But the wine will warm us," she says without waiting for an answer. She removes the foil from the bottle and expertly extracts the cork.

By the time Anna has nibbled a piece of bread spread with ripe Gorgonzola, she realizes that she *is* hungry. The first sip of red wine floods her senses, and she feels her exhausted body begin to relax. Still, a small voice within her asks why this Contessa di San Giorgio is being so considerate. Why the mystery? What is hidden?

As if guessing Anna's uncertainty, Diana says, "Now, Anna, I will tell you what I know." She reaches into a small silk purse, draws out a cigarette and lights it. "I hope you don't mind?" she says, eyebrows lifted in question.

Anna, who has never smoked, might have made a face if she didn't sense that Diana is about to disclose something momentous. She shakes her head.

"The police tell me they suspect that my cousin stabbed your father before he wandered out into traffic—before the bus struck him." Diana stares silently at her cigarette. "Sebastiano could not have been in his right mind," she murmurs. "But the autopsy showed that the knife did not kill your father. The stabbing was what they call a precipitating factor—I think that is the English. It preceded your father's death and was therefore a factor, but secondary." Diana draws on her cigarette and exhales again. "A woman who came forward seems to have witnessed the bus accident itself. She told police that your father was crossing the road, walking toward her and her two children. She said this elderly man, stumbling along with a bandage on his head, stared at her excitedly, as if he knew her. With his eyes on her, he walked straight into the path of the bus." She shakes her head. "The poor woman was very upset, mostly for her children. But she said that your father was a complete stranger to her."

Anna tries to imagine the scene—Anders flirting with a woman across a street, walking into oncoming traffic. Was he that crazy, that desperate, at his age, for a conquest? She studies the intricacies of the parquet floor's geometric design, as if the solution to the puzzle of Anders, the stepfather she never understood, lies beneath her feet. "He had a bandage on his head?"

"He'd had a fall here, upstairs, and suffered what I believe you call a concussion. Our Dr. Corsini took care of him."

Anna frowns. "But why would your cousin stab him?"

"Ah," says Diana, shaking her head. "That is the question. They knew each other for years—such old friends, you know. It is inconceivable." She reaches for her wine, sips it, and sets it down. "Of course, Sebastiano has always been a person of very strict morality. It is possible he may have disapproved at times of certain activities of your father."

"Activities?"

"Anders—you call him Anders yourself, don't you? He had a fondness, as you must know, for the ladies." Diana puffs on her cigarette. "Sebastiano is a bachelor, and although it was not for him to judge, I know he was shocked at some of your father's romantic conquests. He seemed to feel that when Anders brought certain women, some quite young, to stay with him at La Lilia, that this was not quite appropriate. Of course, my cousin has always been, shall we say, sweetly innocent, and rather easily dismayed."

"But your cousin couldn't have been so shocked at my father's behavior that he tried to *kill* him, could he?"

Diana's eyes moisten and she shrugs helplessly. "Who can know? Sebastiano has always loved me dearly, more than any cousin could, and when men become jealous…"

"Jealous?" What is the woman saying? "Your cousin was jealous of my father, about *you*?"

All expression leaves Diana's face. "I can see that I must explain certain things." She leans over the table and taps her cigarette into the ashtray. "When your family rented the house in Greve years ago, I was a schoolgirl. I recall Anders suggesting to my father, 'Federico, why don't you let me teach your Diana some English? It is the international language now, you know.' That is how I met your father." She glances at Anna. "And you had a younger brother, didn't you?"

"Yes, Thomas. He died quite a while ago."

"I am sorry. What tragedy you have had in your family."

"Yes, it's strange to find myself the sole survivor of a difficult family."

"I have come to think that all families are difficult, Anna, each in our own way. But you have your children, and surely you have friends back in America."

Anna sips her wine, appreciating its robust tartness. "Of course I have Katey and Tommy. As for friends, I left them behind in Ohio, where I lived with my husband. He is a professor at the university in Columbus. I decided to leave him over a month ago when I found out about him." She glances at Diana. Will she understand, given that Europeans are reputed to be accepting of mistresses and lovers? "My husband had been having an affair for years, right under my nose. I just couldn't deal with it. I took my children and flew off to Anders' *casita* in Arizona. I needed time to decide what to do next."

"It is a sad story, but familiar to so many wives, no?" Diana leans forward, frowning, to put out her cigarette. "Your husband was a university professor, like Anders?" She sets down her glass to slice more Gorgonzola.

"As it turned out, just like Anders," Anna says, watching Diana's deft strokes, "the father who was not really my father."

Diana offers Anna more Gorgonzola-topped bread. "Yes, I knew that."

"You knew?" Anna stares at Diana, ignoring the bread and cheese.

"I learned of it after Anders mentioned it to me only a few days ago, when we were having a—how do you say—a heart-to-heart discussion."

"A heart-to-heart discussion?" Anna feels oddly struck by a twinge of jealousy.

"Anna, it was a discussion in which," Diana says, returning the slice to her own plate, "certain matters came up about things that happened long ago."

Anna stares at her own hands, noting irrelevantly that her nails need filing. Things seem to be coming at her thick and fast. "Why would my paternity have been a subject of your conversation with my father?" she says, her tone, she realizes, almost strident.

"Oh, it was not a *subject,* as you put it. He only mentioned it in passing. He was explaining what he thought were the causes of the accident that killed your mother."

"*What?*" Anna says, at the mercy of her nerves.

Diana fixes her eyes on the fireplace at the other end of the room. "Why am I telling you these things?" she says. "I think it is because I am the only one, besides my cousin Sebastiano, who can explain things that you should know. And my cousin would never tell you. Even if he recovers from his seizure, he would not, as a man. You should hear these things from a woman, anyway, don't you think?"

Anna does not know what to say. There is something ominous lurking in the background here—something this Contessa is holding back. She shrugs and smiles bitterly. "Well, I don't have much choice, do I? As long as I am here to fetch Anders' body, I may as well hear it all."

Diana impulsively touches Anna's elbow. "But it is less terrible, you know, if you remember that these things happened so long ago."

Anna stares at her companion, resigned to listening.

"Very well," Diana says, quietly, smoothing an invisible wrinkle from her black slacks. "Over thirty years ago, when your family moved to Greve, your father made his offer to teach me English. We had a few lessons right in the hotel. My father trusted him—why? Who knows? Because Anders kept sending guests to his hotel from America? Or perhaps because your father was knowledgeable, with a certain flair? Or maybe because university professors command such respect in Europe. But with me he was a bit of a tease, a sly jokester. He paid attention to every little thing I said, and he quickly—*come si dice*—got under my skin. I recall thinking to myself, 'I should have had a father like this man.' Soon we stopped our lessons in the hotel and started meeting in the Biblioteca. My father thought the lessons were over because of course he was no longer paying him."

"So, you and Anders had an affair," Anna mutters.

Diana gives her a careful glance. "Anna, you must remember, at the time I was sixteen years old."

Anna's laugh is sardonic. "I used to catch him checking out my girlfriends when I was a teenager. He wasn't that obvious, but it embarrassed and confused me at the time." She stares at Diana. "So, maybe you knew my father better than I did. God knows, that wouldn't have been hard. I hardly knew him at all, except for his interest in women—and girls."

"Anna, please. I know this is painful, especially now, just losing your father. I am only telling you these things because I do not know if I will ever see you again. Believe me, I am not inventing idle gossip to turn you against Anders' memory." She hesitates. "There is another reason."

"What is that?" Anna says, unable to hide her sarcasm.

"There was a baby."

"Oh my God," Anna blurts, nearly spilling her wine. "This is too much. Now you're going to introduce me to my what, my half-brother? My half-sister? Not by *blood,* anyway."

Diana sits silent for a moment, her hands in her lap. "Abortions were not possible in Italy in those days. Yes," she says, raising her eyes to Anna's, "I will introduce you. Or if you'd rather not. As you wish."

Diana's expression is so sad, so direct, that Anna begins to shake in spite of herself. She puts down her glass. "Please continue," she says.

Diana's luminous eyes stare into space. "When I became pregnant, thirty years ago, it was unthinkable in Italy for an unmarried sixteen-year-old of a certain social class to have her illegitimate baby or, as I said, have an abortion. In those days you were fortunate if your father didn't disown you, even kill you."

"You make it sound like a hundred years ago," Anna says, incredulous.

"Believe me, more has changed in this country in the last thirty years than in the last twenty centuries."

"What did you do?"

"I was sent away. To the Maremma, where my father had relatives."

"The Maremma? Where is that?"

"It is the southwest part of Tuscany. For centuries it was a remote place of marshes, wild animals and malarial mosquitoes, a place no one would visit, until a few generations ago, without a good reason."

"And you had your baby there?"

Diana is still as a marble statue. "Yes, but there were complications." She glances at Anna. "There was only an old midwife, and she was half blind, not of much help. My baby had her umbilical cord wrapped around her neck, and every time she was almost born—out of the birth canal—the cord pulled her back in again. My baby was blue already from the lack of oxygen when the placenta tore."

Though Diana's voice hasn't changed, Anna can see the pain in her eyes. "Did Anders know about this?" she asks, holding her breath.

Diana shakes her head. "He was already gone, with you and your brother, back to America."

"And your mother? Didn't she help you?"

Diana looks away. "My mother was intimidated by my father—and by the customs of the time. That is all I can say." She glances at Anna. "But I have forgiven her."

Anna nods, though she doubts that she would forgive a mother who abandoned her under such circumstances. Yet how can she know? She has little memory of the mother they called Kate. "So, you're another of Anders' victims," she says, sardonically. "You and I, both."

"Victim? No, I prefer not to think of myself that way. Too proud, perhaps?"

"But you said you were only sixteen."

"There is no excusing Anders. But if I am honest with myself, I was not a total innocent. I knew, even at sixteen, what he was up to, but I was—what shall we say—intrigued?" She sighs. "The one I truly pity is my daughter."

"You say I will meet her?"

"If you wish, Anna." Diana's eyes sadden and deepen. "*Ma senta*, allow me to give you more wine," she says, reaching for the bottle. "Perhaps we can return to the subject of your father. I keep asking myself what Anders was thinking," she says, pouring their wine, "when he was crossing that road, wounded as he was, with his eyes fixed on that woman standing there with her two children on the steps of the Church of San Miniato."

Anna reluctantly tries to conjure an image of the scene, tries to picture the expression on her father's face. "Knowing Anders, he was trying to figure out how he could separate the mother from her children and get her alone for a few minutes."

"So, you think that he was obsessed with seducing women right up until his last breath? Not noticing all the cars and buses on the road that could kill him?"

"It wouldn't surprise me," Anna says. "If the woman was wearing a dress, he was probably thinking how easily it would come off. It's a kind of sickness, you know, like alcoholism or drug addiction."

Diana glances up from her glass, frowning. "He left us in the middle of the night. He found his way down the steps, all the way to the outside doors, in darkness. It is strange. Our nurse, Bianca, seems to think he was not the same after he fell and hit his head after meeting Teresa. He went into the room afterward to see her again, in the middle of the night, after we brought him back from the hospital and put him to bed. Bianca said he seemed disoriented. I think that up there, at Il San Miniato al Monte, he was not in his right mind."

Anna smiles bitterly. "He could have had anything on his mind."

"At his age, disoriented—in the early morning, after a difficult night?"

She sighs. "I shouldn't say these things. After all, he was my father. At least the only one I ever knew."

"And yet Bianca said that he called Teresa, your half-sister—he called her *Santa Teresa*. He asked for her divine help." Diana gives Anna a penetrating stare. "The thought came to me, I do not know why, that on Sunday morning, in his confusion, he might have thought that it was you and your two children, that you had followed him here, that it was *you* waiting for him on the other side of the road at the church. As if...I don't know, as if *both* his daughters were here as holy emissaries." Diana shrugs and smiles. "What do you think?"

Anna feels a pang somewhere deep in her heart. "It is a nice thought, Diana." That is all she can say as she recalls the alluring Miranda Lopez back in Tucson.

Diana sighs and takes a sip of wine. "Anders needed his women, yes," she says. "Still, I think his meeting Teresa, being aware of his part in bringing this daughter of his into this world, in her terrible condition... "

"Yes?"

"When I introduced him to her, and described her tragic existence, he groaned, 'My God, what have I done?' before he collapsed. I believe that at that moment he finally accepted his responsibility for what he had done to her, to you and to others."

Anna is tapping her glass. "Well, I suppose it's possible."

"That would be sad, wouldn't it? To realize your guilt only on the last day of your life, when there is nothing to be done about it?"

"I think of my mother. It was too late for him to apologize to her."

Diana puts down her glass. "I well remember your mother, a tall, lovely woman, though I could not say I really knew her."

"You say you barely knew my mother, yet a little while ago you seemed moved at the memory of her death."

Diana gives Anna an indecipherable look. "I felt...yes, I felt almost responsible for her death, here in Italy, a guest of ours, on our *autostrada*."

"Responsible?" Anna asks slowly. "How could you be responsible?"

Diana looks away. "I was having an affair with your mother's husband, Anna. I sometimes wonder if she found out. What if they were arguing, or fighting in that car?"

"You can't know. You weren't in the car."

Diana throws her a strange glance. "In a way I *was* in that car."

"What do you mean? Oh, you mean metaphorically. Afterwards you felt guilt from your affair."

Diana forces a smile. "Yes, I felt guilt. I still do."

"It was his fault. You know that."

Diana shakes her head and sighs. "You are going to visit the cemetery tomorrow?"

"I'm going to rent a car through the hotel, then take the Chiantigiana south. I looked at a map. I think it's only forty minutes or so."

"It occurred to me that I might drive you myself. I know the area and could help you with the people at the cemetery. I doubt that they speak English."

"Why, thank you." Anna bites her lip. "I'm still not sure about burying him next to my mother."

Diana smiles. "When Dante reached the top of Mount Purgatory he found his Beatrice waiting for him. She had strong words for him about the ladies he had entertained after she died. He had lost his way and forgotten the Beatrice he had vowed to love forever. Your mother may have similar deep-felt words for Anders. She has waited a long time."

Anna sighs. "Yes, she has."

The End

211

Acknowledgements

I have had the benefit of generous commentary on the part of fellow Santa Fe writers Colin Barker, Glenna Boyd, Charlie Romney Brown, the late Marigay Grana, Margaret Mooney, Jim Roghair, Tori Shepard, Tamar Tomson, and the late Margaret Walsh. I am in debt to the late Susan Stern, teacher of fiction writing, and to Lynn Stegner, now teaching writing at Stanford University.

Members of my Dante group, to whom I am most grateful, include Page Allen, Keith Grogg, Anna Jane Hayes, Mary Springfels, Diana Stege, the late Victor di Suvero, and especially, the late Dr. Charles Bell, Professor Emeritus at St. John's College in Santa Fe.

About the Author

In the 1970's I lived in Tuscany for two years with my wife and small son, writing fiction and studying the Italian language at Florence's Dante Alighieri Centro Linguistico Italiano. Returning to New York, I worked for many years in advertising publishing, after which I moved to Santa Fe, New Mexico, where I now live and write. I am a longtime member of a weekly writing group here, as well as a member of a weekly Dante group, studying La Vita Nuova and La Commedia in the Italian. It was during these Dante meetings that the concept for this novel developed, and Florence became the obvious backdrop for a contemporary tale of love, tragedy and retribution.

CPSIA information can be obtained
at www.ICGtesting.com
Printed in the USA
JSHW080847010323
38334JS00001B/10

9 798987 367209